SILVER BROOK

YUMNA AND THE GOLDEN HORSE

SILVER BROOK

YUMNA AND THE GOLDEN HORSE

Yassmin Abdel-Magied

HODDER

HODDER CHILDREN'S BOOKS

First published in Great Britain in 2026 by Hodder & Stoughton Limited

1 3 5 7 9 10 8 6 4 2

A CIP catalogue record for this book is available from the British Library.

ISBN 978 1 444 93462 5

Typeset in Bembo Std by Palimpsest Book Production Limited, Falkirk, Stirlingshire
Printed and bound in Great Britain by
Clays Ltd, Elcograf S.p.A.

The paper and board used in this book are made from wood from responsible sources.

MIX
Paper | Supporting responsible forestry
FSC® C104740
FSC www.fsc.org

Hodder Children's Books
An imprint of
Hachette Children's Group
Part of Hodder & Stoughton Limited
Carmelite House
50 Victoria Embankment
London EC4Y 0DZ

The authorised representative in the EEA is Hachette Ireland,
8 Castlecourt Centre, Dublin 15,
D15 XTP3, Ireland (email: info@hbgi.ie)

An Hachette UK Company
www.hachette.co.uk

www.hachettechildrens.co.uk

To the underdogs. You have more power than you know.

CHAPTER ONE

Oh Allah, please don't let me die!

Yumna's chest heaved. Her breath came out in wheezes, like an asthmatic terrier. Despite the cool dawn air, beads of sweat were racing down the sides of her face. She was hot, stressed and trying not to cry.

Left. Then right. Then left, c'mon!

Gripping the handlebars so tight that the metal threatened to warp, Yumna pushed one pedal down, then the other. Her progress up the mild incline had been glacial. At this rate, she wouldn't hit the peak until lunchtime.

Left, right, left, bismillah, yallah!

Yumna hissed through gritted teeth as she willed her body up the hill. The village was still and quiet, save for the occasional bursts of chatter from birds and sporadic bleats from sheep. She was glad it was far too early in the morning for anyone but the fauna to witness her struggle.

'Good morning, young lass!'

The booming voice came from behind her. Startled, she lifted her feet off the pedals and found herself rolling straight back down the hill. Yumna came to an undignified stop at precisely the point she had begun, outside the weathered front door of her house. There hadn't even been enough time to hit the brakes.

'Oh, hello, Mr Turner.' Yumna spoke with an attempt at breezy calmness, although flames of deep shame were burning up her neck. She straightened her back and smoothed her headscarf, pretending all was going to plan, then turned her attention to the man standing at his gate.

She had only ever seen Turner in formalwear, no matter how early or late in the day they crossed paths. Often, he was in a black suit and waistcoat, but sometimes, like today, he sported the 'penguin outfit'. Turner had explained the fancy costume was called a morning coat, but Yumna preferred to think of him as dressed up like a giant, flightless aquatic bird.

Pay attention.

Yumna narrowed her eyes. The leather shoes had been recently polished. The bronze cufflinks looked large and heavy, more ornate than Turner's usual. Taking in the details, Yumna deduced there must be some special occasion, or someone Turner was hoping to impress. Her assessment had been completed in the space of a few breaths, and she felt far better for it.

The elderly man smiled. 'Struggling on the bike, are we?'

Yumna chuckled, her embarrassment thawing under Mr Turner's warm gaze. She liked her neighbour, the tall man with owl eyebrows who worked as a part-time butler in the castle up the way, officially known as Wenning Keep. He was the only adult – apart from her father – who paid attention to her, who asked her questions, who noticed she was there. Yumna knew she wasn't like her two best friends, the athletic and beautiful Sadeeqa, or the sassy and charming Nafisa. She was a small, stocky thirteen-year-old who spent most of her time buried in books, avoiding conversations with strangers. Most people took no notice of her, but she didn't mind. One thing she had learnt from all the detective series she'd read: you can get away with a whole lot if people don't see you.

'It's my first day on the job,' Yumna admitted. She gestured at the stack of rolled up newspapers packed into her front basket like a bundle of cinnamon sticks. 'Mr Gareth said if I can get Eastbourne Lane done before sunrise, he'll let me do the whole village next week!' Yumna sighed. 'I don't think I'll make it . . .'

Rubbing his jaw, Mr Turner peered at the dials on

Yumna's handlebars. She had remembered the settings from the last time she went on a ride with her father and adjusted them to match. Judging by the expression on Mr Turner's face however, Yumna wondered if she had missed a trick.

'You know how these gears work, lass?'

She shrugged, hoping Mr Turner would not ask any more questions. It was far too early on a Sunday morning for a quiz on bicycles!

'They certainly don't work the way you've got 'em!' Mr Turner chuckled, twisting the dials until they were at the lowest numbers on both sides.

'Give that a go, eh?' Mr Turner stepped back, beaming, and gestured up the street.

Sceptical, but willing to give him a chance, Yumna placed her foot on the pedal with the same amount of force she had been exerting a few minutes earlier. The bike bunny-hopped forward.

'Ay!'

Squeaking like an excited guinea pig, Yumna was off and flying without a backward glance. At the top of the hill, which came sooner than expected now the bike was in the right gear, Yumna paused to yell her thanks to Mr Turner. But when she turned, all she could see at the bottom of the hedge-lined street were curls of soft, grey mist.

⋆

Yumna hummed under her breath as she rode, pausing in front of each house on Eastbourne Lane and pushing the morning paper into the letterboxes, careful not to bend the edges.

The houses on this side of the village were much grander than where Yumna lived. On her street, houses had numbers. Here, the buildings had names, all with matching personalities.

Peacock Manor had an enormous shrub at its entrance, trimmed in the silhouette of the sullen-faced bird. Winterbeck House had a driveway so dramatic, Yumna pictured horse-driven carriages lined up there for the ball of the season. Belvoir Cottage was as much a cottage as Buckingham Palace was a modest family home. The estate was so enormous, it had its own postcode! Fortunately, it only had one letterbox. The round metal cylinder of the newspaper holder jutted out from the brown stone wall beside high golden gates, and she pushed the paper in, pleased at how neatly it fitted.

Yumna's basket was almost empty as she made her way up the final stretch of Eastbourne Lane. The sun had come over the horizon now, clearing the mist and raising the temperature. A wide smile lit up her face as she approached; Yumna had kept her favourite house for last. Here, there was no giant wall hiding the residents from view, or an intimidating gate glowering over passers-by.

Instead, the walls were a low, red brick, gently curving

into a driveway lined with towering chestnut trees that greeted visitors with a warm, welcoming hug. The sweet smell of jasmine hung in the air, and the ground was carpeted in a lush, deep green with bursts of lilac and yellow wildflowers sprinkled across the landscape like confetti.

'The Red Mansion' – that's what Yumna and her friends called Glebe Manor, the old Georgian house that had sat empty for as long as they could remember. It had once been attached to the old church and been the home of the local vicar, but over the years it had fallen out of use. Yumna had often wondered why the grand old residence had been left empty and unwanted for so many years, despite its charm and rough beauty. With its brick walls covered in ivy, its wide front garden and scramble of lawn and woods out the back, it seemed like an ideal home for a bustling family. What would the walls say, if they could talk? Was the house ever lonely?

Yumna dismounted and wheeled her bike to the main entrance, looking for the postbox. There hadn't been anywhere to leave the paper at the foot of the driveway, but she couldn't see anything here, either. There wasn't even a mail flap in the cream-coloured front door. Yumna knew that her boss, Mr Gareth, would ask her if she had delivered each paper to its intended recipient, and she couldn't bear to lie. This was meant to be her gig for the whole summer, she couldn't get fired on the first day!

Parking her bike and perching on the front steps between the overgrown pots, Yumna pulled the rubber band off the newspaper and unfurled it. Flicking through the stories, an ache bloomed across her chest. Gosh, there was so much happening in the world! Detectives catching thieves, children winning chess competitions, ancient treasure being discovered, murders being solved. It was all so exciting, and all so far away. Nothing happened in this village, in this tiny, boring corner of the world. Silverbrook was an invisible place, and she was an invisible person in it.

Yumna wanted more. She wanted to be in the thick of it, following clues like Sherlock Holmes or Nancy Drew, discovering hidden secrets and unravelling knotty mysteries nobody else could figure out. Yumna knew she could do it: she was curious and observant, she could sneak into places and she always guessed whodunnit before the end of a detective novel. But how on earth was she meant to become a detective from Silverbrook? The only real mystery in this village was why they were living here in the first place.

Yumna was folding the paper back up when an advert caught her eye. On the back page, tucked in between two screaming adverts for second-hand cars and farming equipment was a short paragraph. She almost missed it, but it had a magic word in the headline.

FANCY YOURSELF A SLEUTH?

'Yes, yes I do!' Her nose grazed the ink as she read aloud.

Private detective agency looking to recruit young candidates for training. Must be clever, curious and cunning. Send in CV with a cover letter describing a time you solved a mystery in your local area.

There was an email address at the bottom: sleuthmenow@pm.me.

Yumna gasped. This was her chance! Committing the details to memory, she folded the paper back up and left it propped against the door before scrambling to her feet. Being a detective in training was a way better summer job than the newspaper round. Imagine what she could learn, all the tips and tricks of the trade she would be taught. Yumna tried to guess the character of the lead detective based on the tone of the advert. Was it the voice of the sharp but unassuming Ms Marple, or the bolshy and brusque Hercule Poirot? The email address seemed very modern; maybe it was a younger detective, opening up their own agency and hoping to battle it out with the old guard.

Yumna amused herself with these fantasies as she rode

home, letting out a squeal of glee as her wheels picked up speed and the bike raced downhill, gravity doing all the work. She even tried taking her hands off the handlebars for a brief moment, but the thud of the front wheel tripping over a pothole threatened to send her careening over the basket. YIKES! She clamped her hands back down and squeezed the brakes gently to slow her descent. She couldn't slow her heart down, though. It was all too exciting!

It was only once she'd entered the dim kitchen and picked up the note her father left ('*Gone to work, lunch is in the fridge.*') that Yumna realised the flaw in her plan.

She had never solved a mystery before.

'Ya Allah . . .' Yumna slumped on a kitchen stool, jutting her bottom lip out in a pout. She had tried last summer, but that had only ended in embarrassment. This time would be different, she was sure. There had to be *something* to discover in quiet, boring Silverbrook!

'Oi oi!'

A loud knock on the front door, and the voice of a not-quite angel. Nafisa had arrived. 'Hey, Yumna! You coming, or what?'

Yumna sighed. Nafisa was one of her best friends, and also her cousin, since their mums were sisters. The youngest of three daughters, Nafisa was full of 'little sister' energy.

Despite her two older siblings moving away for university, her sense of entitlement had not changed one bit.

'We're going to be late!'

Not bothering to change clothes – she wore black all the time anyway – Yumna grabbed her backpack from its spot in her orderly bedroom, checked she had all her essential items (wallet, phone, earbuds, notepad and pencil, binoculars, magnifying glass) and headed out, locking the door behind her.

'You're quiet this morning,' Nafisa said, as they settled in behind the counter at the local bookshop. The cramped hole-in-the-wall had been there for decades, oozing cosy village charm. With ceilings low enough that some visitors had to hunch, shelves threatening to fall over at any moment and piles of books in every corner, Yumna sometimes thought it looked more like a hoarder's house than a place of business.

There was no rhyme or reason to the space, no organisational system behind the chaos. Customers were encouraged to lose themselves in literature, browse and discover something new. Nafisa's family had been given this place when they bought the grocery shop and pharmacy across the road, and it soon became clear it was more village novelty than serious money maker.

Nafisa, like all her siblings, had been sent to watch the till as soon as she could count. Once her father's job started taking him away from home for days at a time, Yumna joined her cousin at Silverbrook Books. She spent more time reading than she did selling, but nobody seemed to mind.

Yumna shrugged at Nafisa's comment, and her cousin clicked her tongue. 'Don't be like that. I can't read your mind.'

Yumna didn't know what to say. How could she explain that the perfect opportunity for a life of solving mysteries had revealed itself, but she had no idea how to grab it? Nafisa wasn't like Yumna, had never been unsure of who she was. Nafisa was loud and tall, and everyone listened to her. It helped that her family was wealthy; they lived a few doors down from the large bush shaped like a peacock, on the rich side of Eastbourne Lane. She would never understand.

But then again, Nafisa's family had always been good to them. Yumna's father often talked about how grateful he was to his sister-in-law for taking them in when they'd first moved. 'I wouldn't have been able to do it without them,' he would tell Yumna. 'They were so generous, mashallah. Especially with everything that happened with your mum.'

Yumna still did not know where, exactly, her mother had gone. She avoided dwelling on the topic; any thought of her mother felt like touching a raw, throbbing wound.

Nafisa, losing patience with her cousin's silence, began scrolling on her phone. Yumna sighed. She probably would sound ridiculous to her cousin, but she might as well try.

'I wish there was more going on in this town, it's so boring! There are no mysteries!'

Nafisa looked up, chuckling darkly. 'Oh, little cousin. This village is full of secrets.' She cleared her throat and glanced left and right. There was nobody in the bookshop apart from them, but Yumna thought she saw a flash of fear dash across Nafisa's face, before being replaced by a sly grin. *This was unexpected.*

'Haven't you heard about the mysterious figure in the fields last month?'

Yumna's eyes widened, and she shook her head.

'This is why you need to start talking to more people, little cuz.'

Yumna ignored her cousin's jab, focusing on the important information. 'What did the figure look like? What was it doing?'

Nafisa leaned in, her voice dropping to a whisper.

'Apparently, it looked like a monster, huge, with black shiny skin and gleaming eyes. They say it's searching for something. And as of last night,' Nafisa bored her eyes into Yumna's, 'it's back.'

CHAPTER TWO

Nafisa's knuckles rang impatiently against the wooden front door. 'Knock knoooock!'

The house was small, like Yumna's, and the front garden was mostly concrete, with a few meagre weeds pushing up through the cracks. One corner of the yard held the remnants of a failed vegetable garden, old branch stubs sticking out of the soil like the bones of a skeleton rising from the dead. A small BMX bike with a missing front wheel lay rusted against the low wall. Yumna wandered around the square, making mental notes as she stepped over discarded toys. Nothing much had changed since the last time she'd visited, but that was only yesterday.

She turned her attention to the sky, clasping her hands behind her back like she assumed a serious detective would, and assessed the gathering clouds.

'Do you think it will rain before we get to the hall?'

Nafisa rolled her eyes, ignored the question and knocked on the door again.

The sounds of rustling, a couple of loud thuds and some exasperated shouting was audible through the door. Sadeeqa had seven siblings and, as the eldest daughter, she was her mother's right-hand woman, responsible for maintaining order. Whether much order was ever maintained, though, was a separate question. Yumna hoped it was OK in there. Was that Sadeeqa yelling, or one of her brothers?

'Sadeeqa, c'mon. We're going to be late!'

Nafisa's frustration was spilling over. The ends of her recently straightened hair were curling up, and she was shifting her weight from one foot to the other. Yumna sniffed theatrically. Could she detect the smell of rain in the air? Wasn't that a thing? She was sure she had read in a book in the shop earlier that camels could sniff out 'microbes' that led them to water up to fifty miles away. She was no camel, but . . . Yumna sniffed again. That wasn't rain, that was—

'Can you smell that?' Yumna grimaced. Now that she had detected the scent, she couldn't get the acrid note out of her nose. 'Smells like someone died . . .'

Nafisa whirled around. Her lips were pursed in annoyance, but why? Yumna looked closer. There was colour on Nafisa's lips that hadn't been there this morning, the glint of eyeshadow on her lids. *Weird.* They were only meant to be going to choir practice, the same local choir they had been a part of for years. There was nothing special about it, not that Yumna knew. But Nafisa seemed to have gotten done up. Who for?

'Oh . . .' Yumna corrected herself. 'Like someone died of *pleasure,* because it smells so good . . . ?' This was why she avoided commenting on what she noticed!

Before Nafisa could retort, the front door jerked open an inch, before snapping shut. Yumna pricked her ears, noticing the sound of a rattling chain and metal sliding against metal. Moments later, Sadeeqa opened the front door again, an apologetic expression on her round, beautiful face.

'Sorry, girls.' She shook her head and glanced down at her clothes. She was wearing a loose, dark brown abaya with a feathery light brown pattern across the shoulders and back. Yumna hadn't seen this outfit before. Was it new, or a hand-me-down from her mother? Sadeeqa was also wearing a shiny black hijab and black trainers. On anyone else, it would have been a weird look, but Sadeeqa managed to make it look cool. Yumna glanced down at her own shoes, dirty white joggers she'd had for over a year. She had hoped she would have grown out of them by now, but she hadn't done much growing.

'I thought the twins were old enough now to have their own baths, but apparently not,' Sadeeqa said, stepping out and locking the door behind her.

Water was pooling around Sadeeqa's feet, dripping off the edge of the abaya's bottom seam. It dawned on Yumna: this wasn't a new outfit. It was the same beige abaya Sadeeqa always wore, except now it was dark brown because it was soaking wet!

Nafisa scrunched up her nose. 'So, you decided to get into the bath with them, didja?' She shook her head. 'You can't go like that.' Nafisa crossed her arms and turned her back on Sadeeqa.

'Aren't you going to be cold?' Yumna added.

Sadeeqa nodded up to the sky. 'Can't you smell that? Rain!' She flashed her pearly whites and jogged down the crooked footpath to the road. 'You're both gonna be as wet as I am soon. C'mon!'

Sadeeqa was right. By the time the trio arrived at choir practice, Yumna couldn't just smell the rain, she could feel it pouring down her back and pooling into her shoes. They trudged into the dimly lit hall like soaked cats, squeaking and mewling in the cold.

To call Shington Hall an actual hall was generous. It was more a small cottage, originally home to the post office, then an antique shop, and now a community centre. The floors were dark mahogany with walls of rough brick and flaking plaster. Nafisa said it smelt like old people, but Yumna didn't mind it so much. She felt like Shington Hall had character, and maybe a secret or two.

'Girls! You're late.' Their singing teacher bustled towards them, handing each girl a thick, warm towel as she ushered them towards their seats. 'Come on, get dry quickly now, you'll catch your deaths!'

The three rows of chairs set out in the centre of the room were empty.

'You could have started without us,' Nafisa said. Mrs Hardy's face tightened at the barb, but she stayed silent. Sadeeqa elbowed her mouthy friend.

'What? I'm just saying . . .'

Yumna slumped into a seat and studied her shoes, wishing she had brought a book. This wasn't the first time they had been the only ones to turn up to rehearsal; membership of the choir had dwindled since the Pickwood family had moved away, taking half the choir with them. She looked around her at the tired posters on the walls, the wilting folding table in the corner holding a teapot and biscuits, the cups and saucers from 1983. At least the podium was new, or new-ish. It had been donated to the choir in the early 2000s. Newer than the crockery, but still from before Yumna was born.

'Sorry we're late, miss,' Sadeeqa said as she folded the towel, placing it on a chair in the front row. Yumna was sitting on hers, not wanting to soak the seat.

'It was my fault. I had some trouble getting the twins into the bath.'

At the mention of the twins, Mrs Hardy's face relaxed. 'Ah, the twins. How are they doing, those darling boys?'

Yumna glanced at Nafisa, who had sat beside her and fallen into her phone. If her hunched shoulders were anything to go by, Nafisa was worked up about something. She had been acting catty all the way from the bookshop to Sadeeqa's place. Well, cattier than usual, and that was saying something.

'Are you all right?'

'Yeh, whatever.' Nafisa looked up, glaring at Sadeeqa and Mrs Hardy in conversation. 'Just can't believe I ruined my hair for this nothing night.'

'But it's choir. You love choir.'

It was true. Choir was perhaps the only activity Nafisa enjoyed unironically. She had the 'voice of an angel', as Mrs Hardy often gushed. The choir was less a group effort, and more a collection of backup vocalists to Nafisa's solo show. This was why Mrs Hardy put up with Nafisa's behaviour – she was key to any chance they had of qualifying for the County Choral Festival.

Yumna bit her lip. 'Were you meant to meet someone, Naf?'

Nafisa's eyes widened. 'Where the hell did you hear that?'

Yumna shrugged. 'I didn't hear anything, I just guessed.' It was the eyeshadow that had given her away. Yumna never saw Nafisa waste an application of her most precious palette, the pinks and the yellows blended into each other like a glorious sunset on her lids. Yumna silently congratulated herself for her excellent detective skills.

'Who is it? I won't tell anyone, I promise!'

Nafisa shook her head, spraying Yumna in cold droplets.

The front door swung open, letting in a howl of cold air. Umbrellas were lowered, rain jackets removed, and the remainder of the choir straggled in.

'Oh good, you made it!' Mrs Hardy was quick with the towels, but this lot had been much better prepared. The elderly couple, a pair of retired doctors, took their usual seats in the front row, and the family from down the road – not the rich part of Eastbourne Lane, but not the poor part either – also made themselves comfortable.

'You can tell me,' Yumna tried again, but Nafisa was ignoring her now, staring straight ahead.

'Right, that's eight of us here now, enough to start,' Mrs Hardy declared, straightening out her blouse. Her voice seemed to gather strength as she stepped behind the lectern and flicked her fingers, drawing them all up to their feet. Mrs Hardy seemed to transform when she took the podium, as if the role of conductor gave her a sense of power.

'Let's warm up our voices, shall we? Start with La . . .'

As the room filled up with the sounds of *la la la la la la la*, Yumna stole another glance at her cousin. Was she holding on to a secret, a mystery to be solved? Did it have anything to do with the creepy monster in the fields?

The trio split ways for the walk home, Nafisa heading east, Sadeeqa and Yumna west. They walked together in comfortable silence for most of the way, avoiding puddles and humming.

'Mrs Hardy reckons I could qualify,' Sadeeqa said quietly, as they rounded the corner of her street. 'For Taekwondo.'

Mrs Hardy was not only the choir conductor, but the owner of the village bed and breakfast. She knew everyone in the county, knew all the gossip and doled out information like sweet treats. If she thought Sadeeqa could qualify, it was likely she'd heard such a titbit from a reputable source, like maybe the coach who had been spending the last week in the BnB.

'I thought you already qualified?' Yumna said.

'Not for the GB Olympic team.'

Whoa, Yumna thought. The national Taekwondo team.

She knew her friend was good – Sadeeqa had been doing the martial art since she could walk and was the best fighter her age in the county. She made the sport look effortless. But Yumna didn't realise her friend was *that* good. *Mashallah.*

'That's incredible . . .'

'Yeah, but, I don't think my dad will let me,' Sadeeqa said, as she unlocked her front door. 'He's obsessed with me becoming a doctor, not *needing one*, as he always says.'

Yumna tutted. She wouldn't let her best friend miss a chance like this. 'We will find a way. He's gotta let you.'

It all seemed so wild, Yumna thought, as she dropped Sadeeqa home and walked home in the cool night. A light breeze tickled her skin. Her best friend, training for the Olympics?! Her cousin, good enough for County Choir? They were doing what they wanted to be doing, reaching for their dreams. But what about her? Shuffling down her street, Yumna noticed the light in Mr Turner's house go off. He was turning in for the night. Her eyes glanced over the woods behind their houses, the familiar shapes of the trees, and—

What was that?

Yumna wished she had laser vision or a pair of binoculars. There was something there, moving between the trees.

Crouching, Yumna scuttle-walked through Mr Turner's garden to get closer. No, the shape didn't look like a giant figure. It looked like—

'Kareem?' Yumna called out. What was Sadeeqa's older brother doing, creeping around in the woods by her house? And he wasn't alone.

At the sound of his name, the young man, who had been staring at something on the ground, ran.

But that wasn't the strangest part. Kareem wasn't alone. There were two other people who took off, running alongside him. A teenager she didn't recognise . . . and Nafisa.

CHAPTER THREE

Yumna had reached her friend's house early the next morning, right after her newspaper round. It had gone much more smoothly this morning. She only had to stop three times to check her map, an improvement on yesterday's fifteen.

'I need to tell you something,' Yumna said to Sadeeqa. The pair were sitting at opposite ends of the table in the centre of Sadeeqa's kitchen. On one side of the table sat the twins Abdi and Amir, on the other was Sadeeqa's younger sister, Suraya. Both sisters wore loose-fitting nightgowns splashed in bright colours. The twins were in plain white singlets and shorts, their faces still covered in the ashy sheen of sleep, crying out for a wash. Sadeeqa's father, like Yumna's, left the house super early for work, and her mother was nursing the baby in the bedroom.

It was breakfast time, but the scene more resembled feeding time at the zoo. The noise! The chaos! The pandemonium! Cereal was flying through the air as the twins defended an imagined medieval fort with child-sized slingshots. Suraya was trying to feed herself but missed her mouth every time, spreading the creamy yoghurt all over her cheeks. The TV and radio were on in the background, blaring Somali music and Al Jazeera English, casting a layer of added drama over the kitchen. Yumna watched her friend nimbly care for all her siblings: wiping Suraya's face and showing her how to place the spoon into her mouth, mopping up the milk spilt out of Abdi's bowl, topping up Amir's with a gentle nudge to eat, rather than throw, the food. *She was amazing, mashallah.* Yumna had never stopped to notice how much Sadeeqa did, and not once had she heard her complain. Imagine if she had to do this much? Or *Nafisa*!? The thought brought a smile to Yumna's face. Nafisa would try to hire someone for the job before even thinking about doing anything herself. That was, after all, why Yumna was always at the bookshop.

'I can't believe you do this every morning.'

Sadeeqa raised her eyes to meet Yumna's. 'Well. Someone's got to.'

She didn't seem too annoyed. *How intriguing.* Yumna had no siblings at all, it was only her and her father. Quite different from Sadeeqa, who had a large family and was often going out of town to visit relatives in villages and towns further away. Yumna knew her tiny family unit was unusual, or at least, that's what Nafisa said. But it was all she knew.

Yumna didn't remember much about Hull, the town they lived in before moving to Silverbrook. She was born there, and according to her father, it was a fine enough place. After her mother's disappearance, he decided that they couldn't stay and Nafisa's mother suggested they move in with them. Her dad went to work for Nafisa's father, renting out farming equipment, and the two of them settled in quiet, hidden, Silverbrook.

Yumna was only two or three when they moved into the village, but in the years since, her father had shown zero interest in finding another wife. Nafisa's mother was constantly making suggestions, pointing out eligible women in the area. 'How could I replace Amina?' he would say, whenever the topic came up. 'Anyway, my priority is Yumna.'

What would it be like, Yumna wondered as Sadeeqa gently pressed a glass of chocolate milk to Sami's mouth, to be responsible for someone else apart from you? She didn't think it would be such a terrible thing, if her father got remarried. Maybe that way, he would come home more.

Maybe that way, the house wouldn't feel so empty.

'I saw the weirdest thing last night,' Yumna said, trying again. She had been bursting to tell Sadeeqa about what she'd seen in the woods but hadn't had the chance. She didn't have her own mobile phone, and anyway, this was a story that needed to be told in person. She wanted to get Sadeeqa's full reaction.

'What was it?'

Before Yumna could launch into her story, they were interrupted once again.

'SADEEQA!' It was her mother.

'I'll be right back,' Sadeeqa said, now looking harried. 'Can you look after them for me?'

Yumna chuckled. 'Ha, of course. I have years of experience looking after small children . . .'

It was only as her friend walked away that Yumna realised Sadeeqa wasn't joking.

Yumna blinked once, twice, wondering, hoping maybe this was a bad dream she would wake up from. The little kids were all frozen in place, watching her, wondering what she was going to do next. The voice of the news presenter blared from the television, announcing another tragedy in a place Yumna would never get to see.

'Right!' Yumna clapped her hands loudly, startling Suraya into tears. 'Oh, no, Suraya, please don't cry . . .' Yumna reached over to pat her face clean with a towel, but instead found herself smearing more yoghurt across the child's face – she had picked up the rag Sadeeqa had used to clean the table.

A piece of cereal hit the side of her face, and the twins giggled. Yumna ignored them. Another piece of cereal, and another giggle. *Remember,* Yumna told herself, *children are Allah's blessing. They are a gift!*

But when a spoon full of honey went careening into the air, smacking the back of Yumna's head and sticking to her freshly washed headscarf, all Yumna wanted to do was scream. Maybe it was a good thing she had no siblings!

'Going for a walk around the village, Ma. Will be home soon!'

An hour and a half later, Yumna and Sadeeqa got their moment alone. The twins were settled in front of the television, the news channel switched to an animated series, while Suraya napped at her mother's feet. They left the house before anyone could ask for anything else.

The friends made their way up the street, letting the warmth of the early summer sun sink into their skin. The air felt fresh, crisp, and the sky was a clear pale blue, like the colour of winter frost, or Mrs Hardy's eyes.

'So, what's the big news?'

Breathless with excitement, Yumna filled her in. The mystery about the figure, the shadows in the woods and who she saw. Sadeeqa listened silently, not reacting once, even when Yumna finished speaking.

'Can you believe it?' If she was going to investigate, it would be a lot more helpful if Sadeeqa was on board, Yumna knew that.

Sadeeqa took a deep breath in. Her shoulders had crept up and up, almost to her earlobes. As she breathed, Yumna watched Sadeeqa's upper body relax. Then, she shook her head and spoke with quiet, burning fury.

'I can't believe Nafisa is hanging out with my brother.'

Yumna couldn't believe this was the part that Sadeeqa mentioned first.

'Yeh, but there was another guy there also, and they looked like they were doing something shady.'

'Kareem! I can't believe it. He is so . . . gross!'

Kareem was not gross, Yumna wanted to say. Kareem was definitely the best-looking boy in the village, if not all the villages in the area. He had a mop of curly, black hair, cheekbones that looked like they belonged in a museum and the most beautiful skin Yumna had ever seen. But, again, that was not the point of the story! Yumna tried to steer the conversation back to the topic at hand. The mystery!

'The real question is, what were they doing in the woods?'

'You're right.' Sadeeqa stopped abruptly, Yumna almost running straight into her. 'What *were* they doing in the woods?' Her voice had crept up an entire octave. 'What do you think they were doing in the woods?! What does anyone do in the woods?!'

Yumna racked her brain. The only examples of wood-related activity she could think of were deforestation – like they did in the Amazon – and burying bodies.

'I don't think they were doing any logging . . . and I checked afterwards, and it didn't look like they had been burying a corpse—'

'BURYING A CORPSE! Yumna, have you—' Sadeeqa threw her hands up into the air and stomped off.

Yumna was confounded. Why was Sadeeqa so upset? It was very unlike her; she was the calm one in the group. She mentally replayed the conversation to pinpoint what might have gone wrong.

'Oh, sis, wait up! We haven't even talked about Taekwondo!'

Yumna found Sadeeqa on a bench at the village square, swinging her legs. She joined her friend on the wooden seat.

'People always like Kareem,' Sadeeqa said, her tone flat. 'He's the popular one, the athletic one.' She leaned back.

'I'm already on second dan and he's still on red belt, but people still think he's better at Taekwondo.' Sadeeqa's bottom lip trembled.

'But that's not true,' Yumna started, stopping when she noticed a tear slip down her friend's face. 'Sadeeqa! Oh, I'm so sorry!'

Yumna took Sadeeqa into an awkward side hug, letting her friend bury her face in her shoulder.

'I'm sorry,' Sadeeqa sniffled, but Yumna just shushed her, rubbing circles on her back. Once the tears had subsided, Sadeeqa wiped her face with the sleeve of her abaya and blinked up at Yumna.

'I just never would have guessed Nafisa would be into him too. She had always thought he was a bit of a – what did she call him?'

'A plank, I think.'

Nafisa had never seemed to respect Kareem or be enchanted by his charm and good looks. In fact, if Yumna were to guess, she would say Nafisa found Kareem downright annoying.

But then, there was the make-up. The weird attitude, and the obsessive texting during choir, all quite unlike her. Maybe Nafisa had had a change of heart?

'But there was that other guy too . . .' she said carefully. The one Yumna didn't recognise. Maybe *he* was the object of Nafisa's affection. In that case, Sadeeqa had nothing to worry about.

Sadeeqa stood up, her jaw set. She had the same look in her eyes as she did before she had a Taekwondo fight. Yumna wondered if she needed to be scared for Nafisa.

'Let's go talk to her.'

Yumna sucked in her breath. Confronting Nafisa was never a good idea.

'Are you sure that's a good plan . . . ?'

Sadeeqa towered above her, anger lengthening her spine and broadening her shoulders. Yumna felt sorry for her friend's opponents on the mat.

Then, she thought of a better idea.

'What if we followed them? Tonight?'

CHAPTER FOUR

The sound of jingling keys rang out across the kitchen and Yumna heard the sound of the deadlock sliding back. The door swung to reveal her father, a slim man with sloping shoulders, a mop of tight curls and a look of exhaustion etched into his face.

'Oh, Baba!' Yumna rushed towards him.

She hadn't been expecting him home this evening. Her dad had been working late nights for weeks now, and they'd mostly been communicating through notes on the fridge. Yumna didn't mind his absences too much. She found the messages fun, like they were sending each other old-school telegrams. Money was tight and selling farm equipment wasn't easy, so she understood why her father was away a lot. But that didn't mean she didn't miss him.

'I didn't know you were coming home early!' Yumna

enveloped her father in a tight hug. She felt his thin frame stiffen, then relax, as he gently patted her back and murmured his greeting. Her ear pressed against his firm chest, Yumna could hear the beating of his heart, the air expanding in his lungs.

She looked up, noticing the weariness creasing around his dark eyes, the ever-present sadness tracing the downward curve of his lips. Every part of her wanted to bring joy back into her father's life, wanted to see the smile he gave so freely when her mother was still around. She hadn't succeeded yet, but she would keep trying. A seed of guilt niggled at her as she remembered her and Sadeeqa's midnight plans, but Yumna pushed those thoughts aside. He would be sound asleep by the time they snuck out. He wouldn't have to know. She wouldn't have to face his disappointment.

'Good to see you, habibti,' he said, his voice thick and solid as an old oak tree. Then, a slight frown passed across his face. He sniffed. 'Is something burning . . . ?'

'Oh!'

Yumna ran back into the kitchen where she'd left dinner on the stove. A putrid-smelling smoke was filling the room, threatening to trigger the smoke alarm. The pasta packaging was touching the hot element and had begun to melt.

'Let me fix it,' Yumna said, before springing into action. Grabbing a pair of tongs, Yumna snapped up the burning plastic, dropped it into the sink and turned on the tap, a satisfying *hisssss* rising from the wrapping.

After a moment, all was well, and she opened up a window to let fresh air in.

'See! Crisis averted!' Yumna beamed at her father, who had settled at the kitchen counter, watching his daughter with wry amusement.

'Nice work, habibti. Are you sure you don't want to be an engineer? They are excellent problem solvers, like you.'

Yumna peered into the saucepan, still on the stove. The water was on a nice, rolling boil, exactly how it looked on the videos she watched online. A sprinkle of salt, a dash of oil and then time for the dinner!

'No, it's the detective life for me,' Yumna said, sure as ever. 'Are you hungry? I'm making my speciality!' She held up a bottle of no-name pasta sauce with tomato and basil.

'That sounds delicious,' he smiled. 'Then, we can have this for dessert.'

From his worn and dusty black backpack, Baba pulled out a grocery bag. Yumna recognised the sweet, sugary smell wafting out instantly, her eyes widening in delight.

'Gulab jamun!?'

He nodded, a twinkle in his eye.

'Your aunt made them specially for you,' he said. 'They

won't be as good as your mother's, but they're still pretty good. And you know what they say. One gulab jamun a day keeps the bad spirits at bay.'

Yumna rushed over and peered into the bag. Through the clear glass of the food container, she could see the perfectly round dough, golden globes the size of golf balls, swimming in a honey-coloured syrup. She could feel their warmth through the plastic, her mouth watering in anticipation. These were the perfect pre-adventure snack!

'Yallah, why don't you finish up the pasta and I'll get the plates out?' he suggested, as he rose to wash his hands. He checked the time. 'I need to catch maghreb . . .'

'Food will be ready by the time you finish praying,' Yumna ordered. 'Go, go!'

Abdullah smiled as he left the kitchen, and Yumna's chest aching with a tender, pleasant glow.

Yumna couldn't remember the last time she had cooked for her father, the last time they had shared dessert. She had forgotten how much she missed his company. After some cajoling, and two cups of sweet red tea, Baba began sharing funny anecdotes about his job, going door to door in villages across the county, tripping over pigs and trying not to break the client's china.

'There was this one woman who just wouldn't let me leave,' he said, between bites of gulab jamun. 'She showed me into the living room, and it was one of those very English ones, you know.' He waved his arms, indicating piles of stuff.

'Like on those old people TV shows? Full of random things?

'Exactly. The house was so packed with stuff I could barely follow her through the hallway! She had so many lamps, and vases, and little statues of animals, lamps in shapes of animals, and Yumna, each animal had a name!'

'Even the lamps?'

'Even the lamps. She insisted on telling me the story of every single ceramic creature . . .'

She laughed, imagining her father held hostage by an overly chatty grandmother.

'Did you manage to sell her any farm equipment?'

Shaking his head, he chuckled ruefully at the memory. 'It turned out, I had gotten the wrong address. She didn't even have a garden! But,' he sighed, 'it's OK. She clearly wanted some company, and I didn't mind listening to her stories.'

They fell into a companionable silence, and soon Yumna began to clear the plates. After a few moments, the kitchen counter cleared, Yumna sat on the stool next to her father and took a hold of his hands, rough and weathered from years of labour. She paused, wondering whether this was the right moment, but decided to plunge right in.

'You know I love you a lot, Baba, you know that, right?'

He nodded, his expression serene. 'You are such a gift from Allah, Alhamdulilah.'

'So, you know anything I ask, I ask with love, OK?'

At this, her father did not answer, but only looked at his daughter quizzically. She decided to push on.

'Please tell me, what's wrong, Baba?'

He frowned, pulling his hands away.

'Nothing. What do you mean? There's nothing wrong.'

Yumna bit her lip, unsure about her next step. They had enjoyed such a lovely evening together, the first one they had shared for such a long time, and she didn't want to ruin it at all, but . . . something was off. She could just tell that something was bothering him, underneath his stories and chatter. It was in the way he sat, hunched over like he was readying for a blow. In the way his eyes kept darting towards the window, the way he had triple-checked that the doors were locked, front and back. It had been years since she'd seen her father like this. It reminded her of the years after her mother had left. It scared her.

It was also the gulab jamun. Nafisa's mother didn't cook unless there was something seriously wrong. She was a stress cooker. So, if she had made enough food that she had made it to dessert, the problem was big enough that it affected the whole community.

'I can tell you're worried about something, Baba.'

Yumna waited in the silence. The tick of her father's wristwatch filled the space, until eventually, he cleared his throat and spoke.

'A new family has moved into the village. Into the old castle.'

Yumna's eyebrows shot up, intrigued. This was not what she expected.

'Really? Where Mr Turner works?' She thought for a moment. The house had been empty for some time now, after the Earl who lived there died. The old man had never been married, Mr Turner said, so nobody was quite sure who would inherit it. Whoever moved in would be strangers to the area, newcomers who would have to earn their place.

'Have you met them? Do they have kids?'

Baba shook his head, turning to look at Yumna, holding her gaze with a fierce, fatherly power. 'I've known this family for a long time, Yumna. You are to stay away from them. They're not good people.'

Yumna frowned. 'Are you sure? I mean—'

He interrupted, surprising Yumna. Her father was a gentle man. He never spoke before the other person had finished their thought, yet—

'No. Yumna, listen to me.' He put his hand on her shoulder, squeezing once in a firm punctuation of his statement. 'You are to stay away from the Maidstones, OK? Promise me you will stay away from them.'

'Baba, c'mon,' Yumna whined. How could she resist the mystery of a new family?

'Promise me, Yumna!'

Yumna scratched her scalp, then nodded, despite her reluctance to agree. 'Fine, fine. I will stay away from the new people.'

He examined her face for any sign of deception. Seemingly satisfied with what he saw, he released his grip on her shoulder. Yumna smiled.

'Time for *The Great British Sewing Bee*?'

'Ouch! You stepped on my foot!'

Sadeeqa's whisper was loud as they crept towards the tree line behind Yumna's house. After watching their favourite show together, Yumna's father had thankfully fallen into a deep sleep, and she had snuck out to meet Sadeeqa as planned.

'Sorry, sorry, I can't see anything . . .'

She needed to get better at sneaking around in the dark, if she was going to be any good at solving mysteries. How did all those detectives do it? An extreme diet of carrots?

'Did you see where he went?' Yumna asked, both in an attempt to glean some info and to lighten the mood between them.

Sadeeqa didn't reply. She had followed her older brother as he had snuck out of the house and watched him enter the woods, waiting for Yumna to join. As soon as Yumna had arrived, she'd shot off, leaving her friend running behind her to keep up.

It was an overcast, gloomy night, colder than it should be in summer. Every movement of a shrub or shadow caused Yumna's heart to leap into her throat. Sadeeqa, on the other hand, didn't seem bothered by the dark, or by the braying of the wind, or even the prospect of being seen. By the time they reached the yawning darkness of the woods, Sadeeqa was standing upright and casually peering through the trees, as if they were on a regular daytime stroll.

'I think they went this way,' she said.

Even though this midnight caper was her idea, Yumna felt sick. She pulled her puffy coat tight around her body and muttered a quiet prayer as they plunged into the thick line of trees.

'Bismillah, Alhamdulilah, Allahu-Akbar . . .'

Yumna continued to pray as branches cracked underneath

their feet. They were supposed to be silently sneaking up on Kareem, but their footsteps were so loud! The woods weren't quiet either. There was the constant crackle and pop of movement, the sighing of wind through leaves, creatures skittering, unseen beasts yowling—

'There are no unseen beasts, Yumna!'

Yumna realised she had been narrating her inside thoughts out loud. *Oops.*

'We're in Silverbrook,' Sadeeqa scolded. 'The scariest thing around is sheep—'

A sharp crack in the distance cut her off. Yumna's eyes grew wide, and she held her breath.

'Did you hear that?!'

Sadeeqa squinted into the darkness. 'I'm sure it's nothing.' Her voice came out strained, and she cleared her throat, before continuing. 'C'mon.' As she stepped forward into the inky night, Sadeeqa's black abaya billowed around her like an elven cloak. 'I think I saw a flicker of light over there.'

'Sadeeqa, I'm tired.'

Yumna hated the audible whine in her voice, but she couldn't help herself. She was exhausted! Her legs were heavy, and her arms were scratched up from branches along the way. Her right hand was burning from grabbing on to a stinging nettle to avoid tripping over uneven ground. Her backpack, laden with far too many emergency items, including three litres of filtered water and a single person tent that she was sure could fit two people, dug into her shoulders. She had started to sweat underneath her puffer jacket.

They had wandered around the woods for what seemed like hours. While Sadeeqa strode ahead with determination in her eyes, Yumna's conviction was draining away like water in an emptying bath. Maybe they should just ask Nafisa why she had been hanging around Kareem and that mysterious other kid, rather than following them around in the dark. This was quite a lot of effort.

'Ooop!'

Yumna had run straight into Sadeeqa, who stood frozen in place, eyes trained on a point much further away. She didn't respond to Yumna colliding into her, so intense was her focus on the sight ahead.

'Do you see that?'

Yumna squinted. She could just about make out what Sadeeqa was looking at, a bright flash in the distance. In an instant, Yumna's body was flooded with adrenaline, fatigue fleeing her body, leaving her alert, and afraid. Her palms began to sweat. *What a weird place for sweat to emerge from.* Why was she afraid? They were only following Nafisa and Kareem, there was nothing to be scared of . . .

It was a small fire, flickering in the distance. The flames, from what they could see, looked tame and contained, a regular campfire. But no camping was allowed in these woods, and there was no tent nearby. It must be them.

'We need to get closer.'

As Sadeeqa moved, Yumna remembered her backpack.

'Wait,' Yumna said, as she swung the bag off her back. 'I have just the thing . . .'

Yumna scrambled through the bag's contents, pulling items out as she searched. Walkie-talkies, a neatly coiled five-metre length of rope, a pack of ten spare AA batteries, a screwdriver, a bag of zip ties: Sadeeqa's mouth fell open as Yumna spread her haul out across the forest floor.

'What the—? How much stuff do you have in that bag? Where did you think we were going?'

Yumna grinned as she plunged her arm into the depths of the black bag, reaching for an item all the way at the bottom. 'I like to be prepared.'

With a flourish, she fished out a pair of binoculars. 'Voila!'

Sadeeqa shook her head as she grabbed the binoculars from her friend's hand and raised them to her eyes. 'You're ridiculous,' she said, as she gazed through the lenses.

A wide smile of satisfaction spread across Yumna's face as she repacked her bag. This was exactly the reason she liked to be prepared. The binoculars had been one of the first items she had bought with her pocket money, and they were clearly worth every penny.

'The Night Owl Explorer Pro 5X,' Yumna declared, as she waited for Sadeeqa's verdict. 'See how clearly you can see in the night? I know it's a bit green, but it gives you five times magnification, and it has between forty to eighty hours of battery life.' She paused. 'Not that I've used it that much.'

Yumna had not actually used the night vision function at all, but that didn't matter. She fell silent as she waited for Sadeeqa to report back.

She waited, and waited, then cleared her throat, wondering what was taking Sadeeqa so long. Eventually, she couldn't help herself.

'Soooo, what do you see?'

Sadeeqa didn't reply. She simply handed Yumna the binoculars.

Yumna raised the lenses to her eyes. Through the greenish-blue tint, she could see two people sitting around the campfire, Nafisa with her long braid hanging down her back, and the other kid from before, sporting a skin fade and muscles that seemed far too developed for a young teenager. Standing a few metres away from the fire was

Sadeeqa's older brother, Kareem.

Kareem was tall for his sixteen years but, like his sister Sadeeqa, had that lean, athletic quality that made him look more like a runway model than a body builder. He was nice too – perhaps, Yumna considered, because his father had always cautioned him to be: charismatic and charming and the kind of kid who held doors open for old ladies in the grocery store. But he was also a showboat, someone who loved being in the centre of attention, someone who wanted to be the main character, all the time. A great person to have at a party, but more annoying to have as an older brother. He took all the limelight, and Sadeeqa was constantly shivering in his cool shadow.

After a few moments of watching the teenagers, Yumna lowered the binoculars, uncertain as to what she was looking at.

'They don't seem to be doing anything too weird. Maybe they're just hanging out?'

Sadeeqa shook her head. 'Keep looking,' she muttered.

Yumna raised the binoculars back to her eyes and stared. Nafisa and Skin-Fade were deep in conversation, until—

Yumna took a step backwards, almost tripping over her own feet.

'Did I just see what I just saw?'

Yumna looked at Sadeeqa and then back towards the

campfire, raising her binoculars back to her eyes. After a few moments, she dropped them again.

'Did that dude just stick his hand into the fire?'

'And pull it out without getting burnt? Yeh.'

It had looked like a scene out of a movie. Nafisa was sitting cross-legged as the young man beside her had leaned forward, curling his hand into a fist, and then plunged it into the flame. Yumna had expected him to scream, or squirm, or pull it out straight away – even her face had puckered up at the imagined sensation of the heat, but no. He had held it there, before rummaging around the burning tinder and pulling out a glowing piece of coal.

Through the binoculars, Yumna watched him offer the red-hot chunk to Nafisa, who shrank back from its shimmering heat, before throwing it back into the fire. His face had looked entirely relaxed the entire time, as if he were playing with Lego instead of a lump of burning hot timber.

Yumna studied his face, wondering what else she could glean from his movements. Despite his size, something about him felt soft, almost nervous. His shoulders curved inwards, and he moved with the energy of a friendly giant. He looked entirely different to Kareem, who took up as much space as he possibly could. *Total opposites*, Yumna noted, exercising her detective skills. *How curious.*

'Who is that kid?' Yumna wondered aloud. 'What's going on?'

She could feel Sadeeqa shaking her head behind her. 'I dunno. But I'm gonna find out.'

Before Yumna could reply, her friend had walked away.

They were on a formal track now, a flattened path through the brush that indicated a regular walking trail through the woods. Sadeeqa and Yumna walked in single file, Sadeeqa at the front, striding with purpose, Yumna behind her, head down, hands in pockets. She didn't know what they had seen, exactly, but she really wanted to discuss it. Unfortunately for her, Sadeeqa didn't seem up for a debrief just yet.

A heaviness had settled on their little adventure, and Yumna found herself sour with disappointment. Adventures were not meant to make you feel sad, surely! She had to find a way to make it fun again.

Raising her head, Yumna brought the binoculars, now hanging around her neck, back to her eyes.

She swept the lenses across the landscape. They had climbed quite high now, the woods situated on a ridge which overlooked Silverbrook village. She could see the tops of houses, blocks of white and red peeking through the olives and greens of houses and fields. She swept her gaze up and down, trying to spot any nocturnal creatures, voles or owls or even a tiny pipistrelle. No luck. But then, there was a flash of movement—

Yumna dropped her binoculars in shock.

'Psssst! Sadeeqa!' Yumna tried to catch her friend's attention. 'Sadeeqa, look!'

To their right, only a handful of yards away, stood a golden, glowing creature. It was enormous, with a mane that shone like starlight, and a grace that seemed otherworldly. A horse, but not one like they'd ever seen before. It seemed to glide through the trees, as if untouched by reality. Was it a dream, or a hallucination?

'Can you see it?' Yumna whispered. 'It's beautiful . . .'

Sadeeqa, on the other hand, looked terrified. Yumna suddenly remembered Sadeeqa's deep fear of horses.

'It's not going to hurt us . . .' Yumna whispered, but her voice was drowned out by the horse's snorting, then its loud neigh echoing through the woods. It turned to face the girls, raising its front hoof and kicking at the ground, as if ready to charge.

'Gotta get out of here,' Sadeeqa said, her voice low and tight. Yumna shook her head, wordlessly asking her friend to wait. She turned her attention towards the creature, locking her eyes with its unblinking gaze. Its eyes were wild, darting about, foam gathering around its mouth. *It looked frightened.*

'Hey, hey, shhh, it's OK, buddy, it's OK . . .' Yumna edged towards the horse, her soft voice masking her own fear. She didn't have that much experience with horses, but even she could tell this one needed help. What was such a beautiful horse doing outside, alone in the middle of the night? As she closed the distance between them, the horse reared up, neighing loudly, then crashed down with thunderous effect, before galloping towards them.

YIKES!

Yumna squealed, throwing herself to the side. She squeezed her eyes shut as she hit the ground, a sharp rock digging into her side, her backpack thudding loudly as she fell – then opened her eyes just in time to watch the creature soar right over her. She stared, mouth open, as the horse, which seemed to emit light from its body, landed a metre away from her head, then continued to canter away.

Her heart galloping, Yumna scrambled to her feet.

'Holy moly . . . can you believe that?!' she said aloud.

There was no reply. Yumna glanced around. Sadeeqa was nowhere to be seen. Once again, Yumna's body was flooded with adrenaline, but this time it was sharper, scarier than before.

'Sadeeqa? Sadeeqa!'

Her friend had disappeared. Probably run off when she'd seen the horse, or so Yumna hoped. She checked her phone for messages, but as expected, no reception.

She was all alone.

CHAPTER FIVE

It took Yumna *ages* to find her way out of the woods. She might have an eye for detail, but she certainly didn't have a finely tuned sense of direction. By the time she emerged from the trees, it was only an hour before Fajr. She would barely get any sleep before she had to be up for the paper round.

Yumna blew a raspberry with her lips as she trudged through the back fields, sounding not entirely unlike the horse that had jumped over her earlier. What *was* that? It didn't look real, but they both definitely saw it – Sadeeqa wouldn't have run off like that if she hadn't. Not to mention that weird thing that boy had done with his arm, sticking it right into the fire! Yumna wondered if perhaps he was practising a magic trick, and Nafisa was being the magician's assistant . . .

Nah, that couldn't be it.

Not because magic tricks weren't real, but because Nafisa

would never be anyone's assistant. Nafisa was, as she constantly reminded her cousin, THE main character.

Lots of mysteries to solve . . .

Yumna continued walking, her white joggers getting wetter with each step through the dew-covered grass. Soon, Yumna couldn't feel her toes. It was still pitch black, but when she looked behind her, long black ovals were visible in the small circle of light from her headlamp. She was leaving a trail.

The headlamp was classic Yumna. It was an old, heavy thing, an antique she had found for fifty pence at an old jumble sale, secured on to her head with a leather belt 'borrowed' from her father. Yumna suspected it had been used by an old coal miner, back in the olden times. Sadeeqa had laughed at her when she'd first put it on, saying she looked like a character out of *Doctor Who*.

Who's laughing now!

Her phone was long dead and her torch was out of action (it needed D batteries, not the AAs Yumna had brought), so this was the headlamp's time to shine. The only problem was that it totally scuppered her peripheral vision. She couldn't see anything outside the faint yellow circle of light a foot or so in front of her. Not ideal for keeping one's wits about them.

Standing still for a moment, Yumna reached up and

switched the headlamp off, blinking and waiting for her eyes to adjust. After a few moments, she could make out the faintest ribbon of light on the horizon: the new dawn was on its way. Yumna ignored the sharp pang of panic at how long she'd been out of the house and pushed aside the knot in her stomach formed by Sadeeqa leaving her alone in the woods. She simply focused on the violet of the sky. There wasn't much light, but it was enough for her to walk home without the heavy headlamp, and also, perhaps, enough for her to be able to catch a glimpse of a particular creature that Nafisa had mentioned ever so briefly, the *Moonlight Monster.*

While Yumna had not seen the Moonlight Monster in the woods, she assumed that once she was out in the fields, she would almost certainly catch sight of it. These were flat fields after all, where on a clear day you could see for miles and miles. But she hadn't seen a thing. Yumna wondered if Nafisa had made the whole thing up just to send her on a wild goose chase. Trust her to come up with something like an imaginary creature instead of pointing her in the direction of the *real* mystery – like her new friend whose arm could feel no fire! Yumna resolved to quiz her cousin about this at the bookshop later.

Yumna continued through the field, which she knew would eventually take her to Whitby Street. There was a gate behind Mrs Hardy's BnB, and through that, she would end up on the Main Street, which would take her home. When she started to hear the warbling of the first birds to greet the sun – *I hope you get the worms!* – she quickened her pace. Her father would be up to pray soon, and she'd better be tucked up in bed by the time he came to check in on her, otherwise there would be trouble!

She gripped the shoulder straps of her backpack and charged forwards, her steps making a gentle *swish, swish* through the grass. The air was cool on her face, and the damp smell of moisture hung around them. Yumna looked around, her gaze flickering over the horizon, the stretching fields, the silhouettes of houses in the distance. As she glanced down again, something caught her eye. There were long, black ovals in the dewy lawn, as if someone – or something – had stepped here already. She panicked for a moment. Had she been walking around in circles? Surely not! Yumna switched her headlamp back on and looked directly behind her, craning her neck to see two parallel lines of black ovals in the grass, slightly offset from one another, reaching all the way back into the woods. Those were her footsteps. *Phew.* But then . . .

She turned back to the footsteps ahead of her and used her headlamp to trace their origin. They came from the *opposite direction* and continued towards the BnB. Kneeling down, Yumna paid close attention to the shape of the dark shoe print. It was large, like an enormous boot, and the foliage underneath had been crushed so flat it had not sprung back up. *How very interesting.*

As she brought her face closer to the ground, inspecting the grass from every angle, a loud clatter rang out from the direction of the BnB.

Yumna froze. She switched her headlamp off – the light was useless for something that far away – and squinted. She blinked, over and over again, but her vision instead was clouded by starbursts and strange shadows. Was someone out there? Was someone watching? Suddenly nervous, Yumna straightened, switched on her headlamp, and sped all the way home.

As she slipped under her duvet and wriggled her toes to encourage circulation back into her frozen digits, Yumna thought about all the strange things she'd seen that night. Between the golden horse and Fire-Beating-Skin-Fade-Dude, she'd had her fill of the strange and fantastical. But she couldn't help but wonder if her eyes were playing tricks on her, because she could have sworn that as she blinked light into her eyes that morning, she saw a giant monster slipping into the back door of the BnB . . .

★

The next day, the vibe in the bookshop was *awkward*.

Yumna had slept in, missing her paper round and leaving Nafisa to open up the shop alone. By the time she'd slunk in, her hastily emptied backpack slung over her shoulder, it was well past noon. Nafisa hadn't said a word, only raising her eyebrows to acknowledge Yumna's presence and glancing shadily at the antique wall clock hanging above the door. *Yikes.*

Because she'd been running so late, Yumna hadn't had a chance to process any of the previous night's events. Her phone was still dead as she'd forgotten to plug it in before she went to sleep, so she didn't know what the latest was with Sadeeqa. *Had she arrived home safely? What did she think of what they saw? Was it all a trick, or something real?*

Yumna wouldn't have the answers to any of these questions until either her phone came back to life, or she saw her friend for choir practice later on. But while she had started charging her phone in the bookshop, she felt an odd resistance to checking for any messages. She knew that when she did, she would be forced to make a decision, and every option was perilous.

If Yumna had received messages from Sadeeqa, she had three options:

1. Don't read them – that could be interpreted as ignoring her friend, but there was plausible deniability there.
2. Read the messages but don't reply – that was a *hard-ignore*! Two blue ticks and no reply? *Ouch!*
3. Reply straight away – but then, there was the potential for everything to blow up!

Yumna had woken up quite annoyed at Sadeeqa ditching her last night, but she knew Sadeeqa would not respond well to being told off because *she* was still upset about Kareem and Nafisa. The whole thing was a recipe for *drama.*

On the other hand, if Sadeeqa hadn't sent any messages, that would be even worse. Yes, at first there would be relief, because she wouldn't have to come up with a reply, but then she would be in HIGH ALERT PANIC MODE because what if that meant her friend hadn't made it home? What if she'd been missing all this time, or worse – what if she was so mad at Yumna, she was giving her the *silent treatment*?

Nothing was worse than the silent treatment. Oh Allah, the silent treatment! The thought of it turned Yumna's stomach.

Yumna was the kind of kid people didn't really *see.* Most of the time, she didn't mind being invisible: she was used to it, and it had become a superpower of sorts. But that was when it was in her control. The silent treatment was something else. The silent treatment was someone who *did* see her pretending like they didn't. It was someone else choosing to make her invisible. It made her feel not-there, like she didn't matter, like she was barely human, like she was worthless. Yumna really hoped Sadeeqa wasn't giving her the silent treatment.

'So, are you going to sit there all afternoon pouting, or are you going to get started on the re-shelving?' Nafisa's voice pierced through Yumna's spiralling thoughts.

She sighed. She didn't particularly want to re-shelve, but that was the first full sentence her cousin had uttered since she'd walked through the door, so it was progess. She would take what she could get.

'Sorry,' Yumna muttered, 'for being late,'

Nafisa rolled her eyes. 'It doesn't bother me. There were barely any customers anyway.' Her cousin looked her up and down. 'But you look awful, cuz. What did you get up to last night, fighting werewolves in your sleep?'

Did Nafisa know Sadeeqa and I had been spying on her in the woods? This was her chance to come clean and ask all the burning questions racing through her mind. She glanced at the book Nafisa was leafing through, a large, leather-bound tome, and wondered if that could help her ease into the conversation. *Huh.* She hadn't seen this particular book before, but that didn't mean anything significant. The shop was so old and convoluted, she hadn't seen at least a third of the stock they carried.

Yumna squinted, trying to make out the text. '*Creatures of Islamic Mythology*,' she mouthed out aloud, before Nafisa slammed the book shut, heaving it to one side. Her voice sliced through Yumna's train of thought once more.

'So, what *were* you up to last night? Solving the mystery of the Moonlight Monster?'

Yumna bit her lip, weighing up what to reveal. She could go the blunt and fast route – *who was that guy putting his hand into the fire, is he a magician or someone you have a crush on* – or . . . she could bide her time, confer with Sadeeqa then ask Nafisa.

Yumna nodded, putting on a semi-demure expression. She glanced around, then lowered her voice to a whisper.

'I saw it, you know. In the distance. But,' she paused, checking nobody was in the shop to overhear, 'it went into the BnB.'

After a beat of silence, Nafisa burst out into laughter.

'Cuz, you almost had me there! Into the BnB?' Nafisa cocked an eyebrow. 'Right. And I'm a horse.'

Yumna started. *Wha—*

At that moment, the entrance bell chimed. In walked a

couple whom Yumna and Nafisa had never seen before. They were *posh.* Their class was evident in the details of their clothes, the heavy-looking buttons and neat stitching and the way the material sat just right, like the items were made for their bodies and their bodies alone. It was also in how they held themselves, the expensive way they smelt, the easy way they moved into the space. They moved like nothing was new, or surprising, or unforeseen. They moved like they belonged. Yumna took it all in, curious. Perhaps they were tourists, just passing through?

The couple strode towards Nafisa and Yumna as if they had been expected. The older man, about the same age as Yumna's father, wore a dark tweed jacket over a bright white shirt, matching navy chinos and suede shoes. He had a thick head of dark brown hair, classically cut, and a slight tan. He didn't have many wrinkles, Yumna noticed, even when he smiled. It wasn't a large smile, and he didn't show any teeth, but it seemed genuine.

'Hello,' the man said, his voice like a BBC newsreader. 'I'm Hector, Hector Maidstone. This is my wife, Sybil.' He pointed at the prim woman standing beside him, short, with a neat, blonde bob. 'We've just moved into the village and are delighted to make your acquaintance.'

These were the people her father was warning her about! Yumna felt herself shrinking, trying to make herself invisible.

Hopefully they wouldn't notice her, and she could fade into the background.

Nafisa! She willed her cousin to hear her thoughts. *Distract them!*

Nafisa didn't need any prompting to work her charm. She recognised power when she saw it and, in the Maidstones, there was plenty. She fixed a wide smile on her face and gave them the show they wanted.

'Hello, Mr and Mrs Maidstone, welcome to Silverbrook Bookshop!' Nafisa stepped out from behind the till, slipping seamlessly into guide mode. She spread her arms out wide, as if she was presenting a nature documentary. 'This is one of the oldest bookshops in the entire country, and my family and I are so honoured to be custodians of these hallowed shelves for this generation and the many to come . . .'

Yumna watched her in awe. Nafisa had transformed into someone else. Was it any wonder her cousin was the star of the choir? Curls of jet-black hair tumbled princess-like down her back, her tall frame making her appear older, more mature, than her fourteen years. The Maidstones were transfixed, and they hadn't even heard her sing.

'And who might you be?'

Hector was speaking, but Yumna had tuned the visitors out. It was only when she felt Nafisa's fingers pinch the soft flesh on her waist that Yumna realised what was going on. Hector was looking right at her. *Oh, no.*

Yumna stepped out of the shadows, gave a little smile, waved and then silently scurried out of sight. She could hear Nafisa making excuses for her as she descended down the stairs, into the back, back stacks.

'That's my cousin! Don't worry about her . . .'

It was Hector's reply that made her freeze in her tracks. 'Have I seen her before? She looks awfully familiar.'

She heard Nafisa pause, before replying smoothly. 'Oh, probably not. She's lived in Silverbrook all her life.'

A little white lie, but one that Yumna was grateful for all the same. Why did Hector think he had seen her before?

A chill ran down Yumna's spine as she continued down the stairs. Her father had said he'd known them from before, so maybe Hector had seen her when she was young? Did that mean Hector and Sybil had met her mother? A thought occurred to her. *Was it possible they had something to do with my mother's disappearance*? Is that why her father wanted nothing to do with them?

So many questions!

Yumna sighed to herself as she began to collect piles of books from the return trays and place them where they belonged, letting her mind ruminate while her hands were busy. Despite her grumbling, Yumna enjoyed this part of the job. She liked seeing what people were reading, flicking through the books they were interested in and learning snatches of information about topics she didn't even know existed. She enjoyed putting things back into their original place, stumbling on unexpected connections, bringing order to the mayhem.

Yumna sank into a meditative state as she re-shelved book after book, her mind quiet now. Then, as she replaced a heavy book back on to the shelf labelled 'Mythology', a flash of gold caught her eye on a nearby spine. It wasn't a word, but an image of a flying, golden horse.

CHAPTER SIX

'The Maidstones have a son, you know,' Nafisa said, as the pair walked towards Shington Hall for choir practice. 'Otto. But apparently, he's in Spain for the summer. Lucky!'

The arrival of the new villagers had thawed the ice between them, but Nafisa hadn't stopped talking about the Maidstones since they had stepped out of the shop earlier that day.

Yumna didn't respond to Nafisa, aware that her cousin didn't really want an answer, she just wanted someone to listen to her talk. 'They look so posh he probably goes to boarding school or something.' Nafisa's eyes flashed – was that curiosity, or jealousy? 'How cool would that be?'

Boarding school was all very good and well in novels, but in real life? It sounded terrible. Being sent off to some random place without friends or family, being told what to do by strangers, eating the same bland food day after day – *gross*. Sure, their local school was small and not very fancy, but she liked her teachers and enjoyed taking the bus in with Sadeeqa every morning, listening to music while chatting about the latest Taekwondo club drama, or making up imaginary adventures for the sheep they passed on their way to town. She would give them voices and personalities and Sadeeqa would roll her eyes, but Yumna knew her friend did find them funny, because every once in a while, she'd give her a prompt and laugh.

Sadeeqa would look through the bus window at passing fields, point at a horse and a cow and say something innocuous like, 'What do you think those two are talking about?' Yumna would gather herself, lean over and, in a conspiratorial voice, blurt out the first thing that came to mind. 'Well,' she would say. 'Cow is very annoyed at Horse because Horse has been sleeping in her corner of the field, and eating all the good grass. Cow is threatening Horse with Farm Court if she doesn't leave the good grass alone, but Horse isn't having it! Horse reckons the grass is for everyone . . .'

Yumna loved and admired Nafisa, but she knew she could never share such stories with her. Nafisa would laugh at her, openly and without shame, telling her she was being a silly little child. That's what made everything Yumna saw last night so strange. Nafisa wasn't the kind to play imaginary games or be interested in tricks and fantasy. So, what was she up to? Perhaps the book with the golden horse on the spine would have some answers. It weighed down her backpack, slung over her left shoulder. She hadn't had time to look through it at the shop, so she was borrowing it for the night, hopeful that it would reveal some answers.

But there were other, more important questions to address first. Like, would Sadeeqa be at choir practice?

Yumna noticed a silence. She looked up from the footpath, and Nafisa was staring at her, a question in her eyes. 'Did you hear a word I just said?'

Yumna realised that she'd completely spaced out. How long had she been daydreaming for?

'Uhh . . . I'm sorry. I was just . . .' she trailed off as Nafisa shook her head.

'What is going on with you today? First, you're super late, then you barely say a word all day, and now you're not even listening to me?' Nafisa's eyes narrowed. 'You haven't even been on your phone . . .' They were only a few paces from the entrance of Shington Hall, but Nafisa stopped walking and crossed her arms.

'Has something happened with you and Sadeeqa?'

Yumna's stomach dropped. How was she supposed to answer this without revealing everything?

'What did you do, Yumna?' The accusatory tone in Nafisa's voice was hard to miss. Yumna looked askance. Why was her cousin blaming her?

'Nothing! She's just being Sadeeqa!' Yumna tried to emphasise her point by tapping her foot to punctuate her argument, but it came off as nervous. Nafisa kissed her teeth.

'Then what is it then? You two into the same boy?' Her eyes widened as a thought occurred to her. 'Did you tell her you have a crush on Kareem?!'

Yumna huffed. She was tired of being accused of things that weren't true and not knowing where things stood with Sadeeqa. All of this was stressing her out.

'Not everything is about BOYS, Nafisa! Maybe you should think about that, huh?' Yumna crossed her arms and jutted her chin out. 'I know *you* are obsessed with boys, following them around everywhere, doing whatever they want you to do—'

At this, Nafisa's face changed, a storm cloud passing over her expression. Yumna faltered. She wasn't one for confrontation, usually.

Nafisa cocked an eyebrow. 'Go on.'

Yumna swallowed, but her throat was now suspiciously dry. She felt the spindly hand of shame and embarrassment reach up through her oesophagus and grab her tonsils, choking any sound she wanted to make.

'Tell me exactly what you think I do with boys, Yumna.'

Yumna opened her mouth to retort, but all that came out was a strangled *craw*. She sounded like a baby bird, begging for scraps. *Oh dear.* She hated it when Nafisa spoke to her like this. It made her feel so small, so ridiculous. Yumna didn't just want a hole in the earth to open up beneath her feet and swallow her up, she wanted to rewind time and never have been born at all.

Nafisa's eyebrow dropped. 'That's what I thought.' She pursed her lips. 'You are acting super weird today, even for you.' Her eyes ran over Yumna's face, her expression assessing. 'What happened between you and Sadeeqa?'

Yumna shook her head, unwilling to confide in her cousin. If she began explaining what was worrying her about Sadeeqa, she would definitely end up talking about what happened last night, and she wasn't ready to reveal anything to Nafisa just yet. Also, she was almost certain Sadeeqa would want to be there when they found out why Nafisa was hanging out with Kareem in the woods, in the middle of the night. If Yumna went ahead and asked Nafisa by herself, Sadeeqa would never forgive her.

But Yumna still hadn't heard from Sadeeqa, and she was starting to get properly worried. When she switched her phone on earlier that afternoon, she had closed her eyes while gripping the phone tight, waiting for the onslaught of pings and vibrations, a stream of messages, angry and impatient. But it didn't come. Instead, there was a mild trickle, like that on any normal day. A couple of social media notifications that didn't require immediate attention, one from the weather app announcing a fine day and another from a game, prompting Yumna to 'have a go beating your previous record!',with extra emojis.

No texts from Sadeeqa. Her stomach had dropped. This was approaching worst case scenario territory. Either the silent treatment, or Sadeeqa had gone missing. Yumna didn't know which one she was hoping for.

From all her research, she knew the first few hours after a person's disappearance were the most important. If Sadeeqa really had vanished into thin air and she had kept quiet for the better part of a day, she would never be able to forgive herself. But she knew this was unlikely and, if Sadeeqa hadn't made it home, they would've heard about it by now. It was more likely that she was just punishing Yumna. *Ya Allah!*

So she decided that she would wait until choir practice to see whether Sadeeqa turned up before panicking.

'Earth to Yumna?' Nafisa's voice once again. 'Fine, if you don't want to tell me what happened, that's up to you. Just don't come running to me when you want to patch things up. I'm done being the peacemaker between you two!'

With that, Nafisa spun on her heel and stalked into the hall, leaving Yumna on the footpath outside. She tapped her foot nervously, looking up and down the street, hoping to see the swish of Sadeeqa's abaya as she made her way down Main Street. It was still warm and light, the summer sun turning the wide sky candyfloss pink as it made its way lazily towards the horizon. Yumna could hear the faint sound of farm machinery whirring in the background, the occasional bleat of a sheep and moo of a cow wafting over from the fields. A pair of chiffchaffs fluttered in the air, chirping tunefully. Yumna wondered what they were chatting about. What was the latest chiffchaff goss? Did they also see the golden horse wandering through the woods? She wished she could understand them, speak their language. She would ask them about their day, what it was like to float in the sky. Yumna noticed a ladybird crawling across the concrete at her feet, its lipstick-red colouring stark against the grey. She smelt the faint hint of grass and woodsmoke. She noticed Mrs Hardy leaving the BnB on Whitby Street, locking the door behind her as she made her way towards Shington Hall. Yumna observed all this, but there wasn't a single hint of Sadeeqa.

★

When Yumna finally entered the hall for choir practice, she found the room in a tizzy. Rather than the usual calm hum of conversation, there was an excitable chatter among the congregation. A buzz filled the air. Hector and Sybil were standing in the middle of the room, surrounded by curious members of the group, talking among themselves or attempting to listen in to the conversation between the Maidstones and Mrs Hardy.

Yumna felt a gentle nudge at her elbow. Nafisa's voice was low in her ear as the older girl sidled up beside her cousin and took in the view.

'It's like there's a new animal at the zoo,' Nafisa observed, her voice dry with a hint of humour, their tiff of moments ago forgotten. Before Yumna could reply, Nafisa glanced at the door and pulled on her sleeve. 'Oh, look who it is!'

Yumna nearly collapsed with relief at the sight of Sadeeqa's brown abaya swishing through the front door. She tried to read her expression, but her friend's face was studiously neutral. It was the face she wore at Taekwondo competitions when she didn't want her opponents to know what she was thinking. *Alhamdulilah!* Yumna didn't even care about the silent treatment at this point, she was just relieved to see her friend.

Nafisa gave Yumna a little push in Sadeeqa's direction.

'Go on, go talk to her. Whatever it is, I'm sure you two eggheads can figure it out before we start practice.'

Yumna opened her mouth to protest, but Nafisa made a small movement with her head and nudged her again. Then, in an effort to seal the deal, she called out.

'Hey, Sadeeqa!' Nafisa said, her voice carrying over the hubbub. 'Over here!'

As Sadeeqa looked over, her face grew dark with anger. Yumna gulped, and even Nafisa shrank back slightly, the both of them unaccustomed to seeing Sadeeqa's rage directed at them. As she stalked over, shoulders thrown back, lips set in a firm line, Nafisa whispered to Yumna out of the corner of her mouth.

'She looks *mad*. What did you do?!'

Yumna frowned, her mind racing to revisit the events of last night, before noticing Sadeeqa's gaze was not directed at her, but at Nafisa. Too late, it dawned on Yumna that she had been mistaken all along. She had forgotten why they were in the woods in the first place, and now she had run out of time to warn her cousin. Sadeeqa was furious about Nafisa's betrayal. *Kareem*.

'I don't think it's me she's annoyed at . . .' Yumna managed to bite out, just as Sadeeqa arrived. The tall girl balled her hands into fists, placed her feet shoulder-width apart, took a deep breath in, and stared straight at Nafisa, muttering under her breath. *Oh*. Yumna finally understood why she hadn't heard from her friend all day. *She had been working on what to say!* No wonder she hadn't messaged. Writing an angry speech needed perfect concentration. But before she could launch into the tirade, Mrs Hardy clapped her hands together, startling the trio.

'All right, folks. Why don't we get started?'

Yumna breathed a sigh of relief as the members of the choir dutifully filed into their usual seats, Sadeeqa and Nafisa were separated by voice type (Nafisa soprano, Sadeeqa and Yumna alto).

Crisis averted, for now.

She knew a confrontation was brewing, but she preferred not to face it for as long as possible. As they took their places, Mrs Hardy stepped behind the conductor's lectern, Hector and Sybil standing slightly behind her.

'As you may have noticed, we have a couple of new additions to our wonderful choral group.' Mrs Hardy beamed, as if the presence of these new arrivals was her personal achievement. Even her wispy grey hair seemed to shine brighter, as if the very strands were celebrating. 'Everyone put your hands together and give a warm Silverbrook welcome to Mr and Mrs Maidstone!'

Hector and Sybil stepped forward and raised their hands in a royal-like wave as the soft patter of applause filled the hall. They seemed very comfortable being the centre of attention, Yumna noticed. Even here, surrounded by people their own age, the Maidstones seemed to position themselves as slightly above everyone else, as if the space was being blessed by their very presence. It was an odd feeling. Yumna wasn't quite sure how that had happened, and it didn't necessarily feel like a good thing. She thought of her father's warning again. *Promise me you will stay away from them.* She wondered if Nafisa had been given the same warning by her parents. Her mother had been stress cooking, surely that was warning enough? She resolved to ask Nafisa later, before turning her attention back to the couple standing like visiting dignitaries.

'We are extremely glad to be spending some more time here in Silverbrook,' Hector was saying. 'We've been travelling for many years now, our business taking us across the globe, but we always knew we would want to come back home, back to the glorious green and pleasant lands of England.' Hector looked at his wife and smiled warmly, and Yumna swore she heard Jan whimper with pleasure from the soprano section. It was all so perfect, Yumna thought. *Too perfect.* Then she caught herself. Maybe she was overthinking things.

'When we received the phone call about Wenning Keep, we couldn't quite believe our ears. It is not every day one is bestowed with such a gift – the custody of a fourteenth-century castle.' Sybil had taken over the story now. Her voice was thin and reedy – a soprano, but a weak one, Yumna thought. Though she knew she shouldn't judge, given her own middling ability to hold a tune. 'To be perfectly honest with you all, we weren't entirely sure if it would be the right fit. We'd not spent much time in Lincolnshire, as I'm from Norfolk, and we'd certainly not looked after such a grand estate before.' There was a slight note of apology in her voice, but was it genuine, or a performance? 'Would Silverbrook be right for us? Would Wenning Keep be the right place for Otto, when he came home? Well –' she clasped her hands together – 'When we finally did visit, we knew the answer straight away.'

'It was perfect.' Hector picked up the thread again. This pair was a well-oiled machine, and Yumna imagined even their scoldings were delivered together. 'Although it needed, as you can imagine, a little bit of work.' His voice had that characteristic English wit, dry as tinder. Everybody knew Wenning Keep was falling apart. The old Earl had spent most of his life shuffling between three rooms in the entire building.

'So, while we oversee the Keep renovations, we are delighted to be taking up residence in Glebe Manor.' The bright smile flashed again.

Say what? Had she heard correctly? The Maidstones were moving into the Red Mansion?

'Living in Glebe Manor will allow us to get to know you all, before we sequester ourselves away behind those giant walls on the hill,' Hector said lightly, as if he wasn't talking about the age-old tradition of aristocracy. 'We are so looking forward to becoming part of this community and are ever so keen to do our part here.'

'Take, for example, Shington Hall.' Hector gestured to the building around them. 'I've spoken to Mrs Hardy here about the refurbishment. It's time this wonderful artefact was brought back to its former glory.' Yumna noticed Mrs Hardy's smile from behind him, a woman unable to believe her luck. 'And Sybil, who is an absolute magician with catering and events, has already begun drawing up plans for a brand-new village fete!' There were a couple of gasps of delight from the choir. 'Given some time and under Sybil's guidance, it might just become the most popular event of the spring calendar across the whole of Lincolnshire!'

Yumna could tell that this was not what the villagers expected. It was rare to have newcomers; Yumna had hardly seen anyone move into town since they'd arrived. But rarer still, she imagined, that new people who moved in were so rich and so *generous.*

'Who knows,' Mrs Hardy interjected, her giddiness unable

to be contained any longer. 'If the refurbishment is as grand as Mr Maidstone has suggested it could be, Silverbrook might end up being the host of the next county choral choir competition!'

Applause now erupted, and there were even a few whoops. The Maidstones took their places in the choir while lightly waving away the praise, Hector a baritone, Sybil a soprano. *No surprises there.*

'Looks like they have some money to throw around,' Nafisa muttered under her breath, to no one in particular. *Indeed . . . but why?* Did they really just want to help?

It was the most fun they'd had at choir practice for months. Yumna momentarily forgot about the tension with Sadeeqa and Nafisa as she was swept up in the excitement of Mrs Hardy and her fellow singers. They played with a couple of new contemporary songs and did a whole twenty minutes of improvised harmonisation. The whole afternoon had been a huge boost, and by the end, Yumna felt like she could be on a world stage, singing backup vocals for a power ballad and snapping her fingers like a gospel singer from the 60s.

But as soon as they'd finished up and the rest of the choir had filtered out of the hall towards their respective homes, reality rushed back like a tsunami. Yumna had dragged her feet, hoping that maybe by the time she walked through the doors both her friend and cousin would have already hashed it out, but she was not so lucky. When she finally emerged from Shington Hall, waving goodbye to a still-bubbling Mrs Hardy, they were waiting.

'Look, she's here now. Can you finally tell me what's going on?' Nafisa sounded exasperated as she stared at a tight-lipped Sadeeqa, who unfolded her arms.

'Fine, but not here.' She started walking away, shaking her head and muttering to herself.

'Where are you going?' Nafisa looked at Yumna, who shrugged. She was getting used to Sadeeqa striding off unnecessarily.

Sadeeqa had the longest legs of the trio, so they had to jog to catch up to her. She didn't stop walking until she reached the edge of Main Street, crossed the strip of grass behind the houses, and ended up at the tree line. When she arrived, Sadeeqa turned around and glared at Nafisa.

'Explain yourself.'

Nafisa looked irritated. 'What are you talking about? If you're annoyed with Yumna about something, sort it out with her, don't bring me into it.'

'Why are *you* hanging with my brother?' Sadeeqa snapped. Yumna gulped, *that was one way to do it.*

'Excuse me?' Nafisa's voice was meant to be neutral, but there was an audible edge.

'I saw you. Last night. With my brother. We both did.' Sadeeqa pointed at Yumna, who for the second time that day, wanted to disappear. 'We followed you into the woods and saw you hanging out with my brother and some other kid.'

'You were following me?' Nafisa was properly angry now. She glanced at Yumna, her eyes flashing with fury. 'Is this why you were late this morning? Because you were out late, spying on me? What on earth is wrong with you two? Don't you have anything else better to do?'

'I thought you were OUR friend. MY friend, not my stinking brother's!' Sadeeqa's voice pitched up, the hurt obvious.

'Well, friends don't spy on friends, do they?'

'Why didn't you tell us then? What's my brother got that we don't? Huh? What's the big secret?!' Sadeeqa raised her voice and Yumna winced.

'You're such a crybaby, Sadeeqa. I can hang out with whoever the hell I want to and if that includes Kareem, then you just have to deal with it.'

'So you're just abandoning us because you feel like it? What, so you never actually cared about us, you were just waiting till someone better came along? Was that it?' Sadeeqa huffed. 'I always knew you were a selfish cow.'

Oh. My. God!

Nafisa clenched her fists.

'Wow . . .' she said, drawing out the single syllable. 'Nice. Maybe he is the better sibling after all.'

Yumna was hardly breathing, the tension sky high. She waited for Sadeeqa's retort, but strangely, her friend had dropped her gaze. She was staring at the ground, lips moving, as if she was talking to herself. *C'mon, say something!* The moment stretched, but Sadeeqa remained silent.

'Hello? Earth to Sadeeqa???'

No response.

Eventually, Nafisa screwed up her face and threw her hands up in the air.

'Fine, whatever! Be a weirdo! I don't want to hang out with you losers anyway!'

Nafisa stormed off, back towards the main street of the village.

What just happened?

Yumna forced air into her chest, trying to breath normally and thinking through how best to help. Sadeeqa was still staring at the ground, as if in a trance. Yumna approached tentatively, but when she gently touched her friend's shoulder, Sadeeqa's head jerked up and, for a moment, her eyes were completely white. There were no pupils, no irises, nothing. Just the spooky blankness of an empty sheet of paper.

Yumna gasped. Sadeeqa blinked and her eyes had returned back to their normal brown. When she spoke, she sounded like she had just woken from a nap.

'Hey . . . hey, what happened? Where did Nafisa go? I wasn't done!'

Yumna stared at her friend. What on *earth* was going on?

CHAPTER SEVEN

Yumna had a terrible night's sleep. She had tossed and turned and when the sound of the rooster came through her window at way too early in the morning, she gave up on trying to get any shut-eye. She threw off her blanket and hauled herself out of bed. If she was up, she might as well do the paper run.

It was so early that her father was still asleep, so Yumna tiptoed past his room before letting herself out the front door. She was so lost in her own world, she almost ran over Mr Turner with her bike.

'Whoa there!' he said, and she'd hit the brakes, coming to a stop right by his shiny shoes. 'Looks like you've gotten a handle on your steed now, eh?'

Yumna gave him a half-hearted smile. All her energy was focused on sorting out the thoughts in her mind and small talk seemed like too much work. Mr Turner, ever the observant neighbour, considered her exhausted face and turned to a new subject.

'You seen the new arrivals?' His voice was light, but Yumna picked up a curious note in his voice. She nodded in reply.

'Do you know anything about them, Mr Turner?' Her voice sounded strangely croaky, this being the first time she'd spoken since her friends had argued last night.

Mr Turner sighed. 'Not exactly, no . . . though they seem polite enough.'

He gazed into the distance and Yumna waited. He looked like he was gearing up to say something important, if she had the patience for it.

Birdsong warbled all around them, and the bright sparkle of the morning star twinkled in the clear sky, planet Venus winking at them from afar. Yumna suppressed a shiver. It was always chilly at this time of morning, even in deep summer, but if she wore anything thicker than a long-sleeved shirt she would be soaked in sweat as soon as she reached the top of the hill.

'Polite doesn't mean much though, does it,' Mr Turner eventually said, meeting Yumna's eyes meaningfully. 'Folks like them, they're taught to be polite, even when they're cutting you down to size. It's their actions you gotta watch for. They're all like magicians. Keep you distracted over here.' He brought one hand up near his face and waved it, 'while doing what they really mean to be doing over here.'

Mr Turner brought out the hand that was behind his back, revealing three copies of the morning's paper, which he had taken from right under Yumna's nose at some point in the conversation.

Yumna looked up in surprise. *When had he done that, and more importantly, how had she not noticed?*

Mr Turner's eyes were grey in the low light. 'It's all about paying attention to what people are doing, little lass. Not what they're saying.' He tapped the side of his nose, then strode off in the direction of the castle, melting away into the distance.

Yumna frowned as she tried to understand what Mr Turner meant, but it was too early and her mind was still creaky with fatigue. She put her foot to the pedal and pushed the mess of thoughts away.

Cycling back after the paper round, Yumna stopped outside Sadeeqa's house. She dismounted and leaned the bike against the front wall, her eyebrows knotted together in thought. The sun was fully up now, bright and yellow against a pale blue sky.

Yumna had gone at a leisurely pace this morning, the run taking almost double the time it usually did. She used the time on her bike to chew over everything that had happened. Nafisa, Kareem and the strange boy in the woods, sticking his hand in the fire. A mysterious golden horse. The Moonlight Monster, walking into the BnB. The arrival of the Maidstones. The warning from her father. Sadeeqa's strange reaction to Nafisa last night, her trance-like state, her silence the whole way home. Yumna had *a lot* on her mind, it was no wonder she couldn't sleep. Fortunately, the paper run was smooth and uneventful.

Well, except for one thing.

This morning was the first time she had ever seen the Glebe Manor occupied.

The building had looked, for all intents and purposes, exactly the same as it always did. The same red brick, the same thick, towering trees. Sure, there was now a sleek black Land Rover parked out the front, and the barks of at least two different dogs had rung out as Yumna had cycled up the driveway that morning. But no, the difference wasn't physical. It was more . . . Yumna searched for the word. *Spiritual?* It felt like the house was trying to warn her.

Maybe she was reading too much into it. She wondered if her father's warnings were getting to her head. After all, Sybil had opened the door, just as Yumna was pushing the paper into the letter flap. The prim woman's lips were painted a pale pink, and the sunlight caught on her simple pearl necklace as she offered a kindly smile and invited Yumna in for breakfast. She had graciously declined, of course.

Watch their actions, Mr Turner had said. Well, their actions had been nothing but generous, so far . . .

Mr Sulaiman, Sadeeqa's dad, pushed open the door as Yumna walked up the front path. He was on his way out.

'As-salamu-alaykum,' he said, nodding a greeting as he passed, looking about as preoccupied as he always did. Sadeeqa's dad was a wiry man, bald with a small tuft of white hair sprouting out of his chin like a desert scrub. His skin was a rich, dark brown, and he moved like a Kenyan marathon runner – athletic, but as if he had a long, long way to go. As he reached the front gate, Mr Sulaiman turned around.

'Yumna,' he called.

'Yes, Uncle?'

'Is everything all right with Sadeeqa?'

Yumna froze at the threshold of the front door. Had he seen Sadeeqa sneak back in after their midnight adventure? Had she said something about Kareem, or Nafisa?

'I . . .' Yumna began uncertainly, then cleared her throat. She pulled her sleeves down her forearms – she had pushed them up while cycling, to cool down as the morning warmed up – and tried to look presentable. 'I think so, Uncle. Why, did she say something?' She fished for clues, trying to keep any worry from her face.

He shook his head. 'I was just wondering. Thank you.' Mr Sulaiman looked lost in thought as he used his middle finger to push his glasses up his face and adjusted his grip on the briefcase handle. Yumna knew Sadeeqa's dad had a job in an office, but what office and what he did there was a complete mystery.

'It's just, she hasn't left her room today.' He cleared his throat. 'Her mother is feeling unwell, so . . .' Yumna nodded, understanding. It must be extra chaotic in the Sulaiman house!

Mr Sulaiman turned to leave, paused, then turned back. He spoke like a man under duress. 'If . . . if it's . . .' He coughed, uncertain, avoiding Yumna's eyes.

'Yes, Uncle?'

Mr Sulaiman looked pained, and Yumna had to step forward to hear him speak.

'If it's womanly things, can you please help her? She won't talk to me about it.'

Yumna stifled an awkward laugh, trying to imagine Mr Sulaiman sitting down to talk about periods with Sadeeqa. It was quite sweet, but she knew her friend would be mortified!

She nodded politely. 'I'll take care of her, Uncle. Inshallah.'

With a look of utter relief, Mr Sulaiman all but fled the scene.

He needn't worry. Yumna knew Sadeeqa had gotten her period for the first time this month, and Nafisa had started getting periods earlier this year. She was the only one left with no spotting to boast of. *Soon it will come*, she prayed. *Inshallah.*

Inside, Yumna found the chaos Mr Sulaiman had warned her about. The twins were throwing around as much breakfast as they were eating, and the baby's wails poured out of the main bedroom. Yumna tiptoed her way through, avoiding the younger siblings, fallen Lego and the flying cereal, to reach Sadeeqa's room.

While she technically shared her room with her younger sister, in reality, this was Sadeeqa's territory. The room was always painstakingly neat, possibly the only part of the house that was kept this orderly at all times. Shelves of Taekwondo trophies lined the walls, banners and belts and monuments of all sorts arranged neatly, on every empty bit of shelf space. The top bunk bed was expertly made, the dark blue duvet tucked in around the mattresses, the pillows professionally fluffed. A perfectly folded prayer mat, slightly threadbare from use, lay on one end of the bottom mattress. Underneath the window that looked out to the street, on to the view of the small, concrete courtyard, was a modest desk, where a laptop lay charging.

'Sadeeqa?' called Yumna, as she walked into the room. Her friend was usually on the floor, practising moves, or sitting at the desk with her back to the front door. But the room looked empty.

'Hello?'

Yumna closed the door behind her and listened. She could just make out quiet sniffling from the direction of the bunk bed. Her friend was squeezed into the back corner of the bottom bunk, wrapped up in her duvet, crying into her hands.

'Sadeeqa? Hey, what's going on?'

Yumna crawled on to the mattress and tried to hug her friend, but it was awkward. Sadeeqa was all hard edges and long limbs, and curled up as she was in the corner, it was tricky for Yumna to move into a comforting position.

'Do you want a tissue?' Yumna asked, giving up on the hug. Her friend simply shook her head and used the hem of her pyjamas to wipe her eyes.

'Yumna, I think . . . I think something's wrong.' Sadeeqa dropped her hands. Her eyes remained closed, tears still leaking out from under the lids.

'What are you talking about?' asked Yumna. She had never seen Sadeeqa this upset before. *What could be upsetting her this much?* 'If you're thinking about Nafisa and Kareem, or even the guy who put his arm in the fire, I've been thinking—'

'Forget that!' Sadeeqa shook her head violently. 'This is not about any of that, whatever we saw.' She sniffed again, then slowly opened her eyes, raising her gaze to meet Yumna's.

Ya Allah, Bismillah, Allahu Akbar! Yumna did not know how else to react but to pray. Her friend's eyes were *completely white.* So she hadn't imagined it!

'I looked online. I think it might be cataracts?'

'Cat-a-who?' Yumna wasn't sure she'd heard right.

'Cataracts. It happens to like, old people.'

'Oh, so you have the eyes of a grandma now?'

But her attempts to lighten the mood fell flat.

'*Yumna!*' Sadeeqa whispered, fierce and afraid. 'This isn't a joke! I've turned into a *monster.*' She grabbed Yumna's arms and looked right into her face. Yumna did her best not to recoil, but the all-white eyes were quite disturbing.

'The worst part is, I've got all these voices in my head! They're so LOUD and they won't stop, no matter what I do!' Sadeeqa released her grip on Yumna's arms, leaving hot red welts in her wake. She turned away, facing the back corner of the wall as she spoke.

'I don't know what's happening to me and, Yumna, I'm scared . . .'

CHAPTER EIGHT

'There's a perfectly normal explanation, I'm sure of it,' Yumna said.

After Sadeeqa had confessed, Yumna had spent most of the morning trying to soothe her friend, assuring her everything would be fine.

'Maybe this is what happens when you get your period,' she had joked, but that did not seem to offer Sadeeqa any solace. Yumna did a cursory online search to see if white eyes and hearing voices in your head were something that happened when someone hit puberty, but the internet was not very helpful. Looking up 'Why am I hearing voices in my head' only sent her to websites about auditory hallucinations and forums on mental health. Yumna was almost certain that wasn't it, but . . .

'Did you find anything useful?' Sadeeqa asked, her eyes

closed again. She had explained to Yumna that she could see through the white haze just fine but preferred to keep her eyes closed as there was so much noise in her head.

'Not really,' Yumna admitted, and Sadeeqa groaned. This was going to be one of those problems where the internet couldn't help them.

'What are we going to do?!'

Yumna scrambled off the bed and flung open a nearby wardrobe.

'Hey!' Sadeeqa's eyes were still closed but she seemed to know exactly where her friend was. 'Are you using this moment to steal all your favourite clothes?'

Yumna gasped in mock shock. 'Me? Sis, how low do you think I would stoop?'

In fact, Yumna had already considered the possibility, only dismissing it because Sadeeqa was too tall for them to share clothing. *Such a shame*, Yumna thought, as she fingered the sleeve of a floor-length leather jacket Sadeeqa had bought for eight quid at the vintage market last summer. It paired perfectly with multiple abayas.

Soon, Yumna found what she was looking for. She grabbed the white-framed sunglasses and awkwardly pushed them on her friend's face.

'Wear these,' she ordered, before grabbing Sadeeqa's hand to pull her off the bed. 'And get dressed.'

Sadeeqa grumbled, not wanting to move. She let her weight sink down into the mattress as Yumna strained. Only one of them trained in the dojo every day, and it was showing.

'I don't want to go . . . Where are we going, anyway? I can't go anywhere like this.'

Yumna smiled, keeping her voice bubbly. 'It's a surprise.'

Sadeeqa frowned behind the sunglasses, and she wrenched her arm back.

'Where are we going?'

Yumna sighed. 'We're going to see Nafisa.'

'What!?' Sadeeqa barked, part shock, part fury. She pushed herself back into the corner. 'No way. Nooo way!'

'Who else are we going to go to? Your mum?' Sadeeqa's face twisted at the suggestion. 'Exactly. Nafisa is the only one we can trust!'

Sadeeqa ripped her sunglasses off, and to Yumna's surprise, her eyes had returned to their usual dark brown. Still, they were flashing with anger.

'But we can't trust her!'

Yumna felt like stamping her feet in frustration. 'Just because she's hanging out with your "hot" brother,' she said, pre-emptively dodging a slap she knew was coming her way, 'doesn't mean she can't be trusted. Come on!' In a sudden burst of energy, Yumna grabbed Sadeeqa's arm and *pulled*, taking her tall friend by surprise and hauling her to her feet. 'Get dressed, let's go!'

Yumna stood outside the bookshop, her hand on the doorknob. 'You can fight afterwards, OK?'

Sadeeqa huffed, but did not argue. Nodding, Yumna pushed the door in, the tinkle of the bell announcing their entrance.

'Welcome to our bookshop . . .' Nafisa's bright, bookseller voice trailed off as she registered Yumna and Sadeeqa. 'Hey, what are you doing here? You're not working today, are you?'

Yumna shook her head. 'No, I brought Sadeeqa because we have to tell you something . . .'

'KAREEM?!'

Sadeeqa's voice came like a roar from behind her, and Yumna realised that in her haste to speak to Nafisa, she hadn't noticed there were others in the bookshop. Leaning on the shelves across the till stood Kareem and his mysterious new friend. *Oh dear.*

Kareem's face broke into a cheeky smile at the sight of his sister, while his burly friend looked awkward, staring straight at the floor, as if he wanted nothing more than to disappear. *I feel you*, Yumna thought.

'Looks like you're busy . . .' she backtracked, literally

walking backwards in an effort to get out of there as quickly as possible. She knew it would be difficult to get Sadeeqa and Nafisa to talk to each other, but she hadn't anticipated Kareem being on the scene. Now, it would be downright impossible. 'Come on, Sadeeqa, we can come back—'

Yumna didn't have a chance to finish her sentence. Sadeeqa launched herself at her brother, as if they were in the final round of a Taekwondo tournament. Kareem side-stepped neatly – he might not have Sadeeqa's skills, but he had common sense. Sadeeqa's momentum carried her past Kareem and into the 'History' aisle. They all heard her collide with the Lonely Planet stand and Skin-Fade grimaced as loud thuds echoed through the bookshop.

'Hey, little sis,' Kareem drawled, ever the sweet talker. He peered down the aisle. 'You need any help back there?'

A furious scream came back in response. Kareem lifted his shoulders in a shrug, gesturing as if to say, *Siblings, eh?*

'You're lucky there are no other customers,' Nafisa observed.

'There are almost never customers,' Yumna replied. Nafisa rolled her eyes.

'What are you doing here anyway?' Yumna turned to Kareem, before turning to his friend. 'And who are *you*?'

'I'm nobody,' the stocky teenager muttered.

'It's OK, Sami,' Nafisa interjected, her voice reassuring. 'She's my cousin.'

Sami looked up. 'Oh, hi. Sorry.' His deep voice was bashful, sweet almost. Yumna noticed his long eyelashes, lending his face a feminine quality that was in stark contrast to his thick, muscular physique. From afar, Yumna had imagined he was a typical 'tough' lad, but on closer inspection, it was clear he was a little more complicated than that. *Interesting.* She wanted to ask about the whole reaching-into-fire thing, but given the soap opera unfolding around them, it wasn't quite the right time.

'Oi!' Nafisa interrupted Yumna's musing. 'What are *you* both doing here?'

Before Yumna could reply, Sadeeqa stumbled back into view. She stood facing her brother, then looked at Sami with menace, before whirling to screw her face up at Nafisa, who had stepped out from behind the till. Yumna could see what was about to happen from a mile off. Sadeeqa was going to say something hurtful, Nafisa would reply with something mean and Kareem would add some smart but explosive quip. Both the girls would turn on him and at some point someone was going to throw a book. Or a punch. Not only would it make a real mess of the bookshop, it would also leave their questions unanswered. So, before Sadeeqa could utter a word, Yumna stepped between her and Nafisa.

'Sadeeqa's eyes keep going all white and she's hearing voices in her head and she's too scared to ask for help,' Yumna blurted out in one breath.

Sadeeqa froze, then gave Yumna a warning look. *Don't give everything away at once*, it said. OK, fine.

Yumna looked at her cousin, certain Nafisa's face would be incredulous. She didn't think Nafisa would know what to do, either, but they had to try.

Nafisa wasn't even looking at her. She was staring at Kareem and Sami, right over Yumna's head. Her expression? It wasn't one of incredulity, or ridicule. It was one of *excitement.*

'How long have you been hearing these voices?' Kareem asked his sister. Sadeeqa looked annoyed by his question. She hadn't wanted to hear from her brother.

'What's it to you?'

'Just answer him,' Nafisa said, her voice both elated and exasperated. It was almost as if they were expecting this, Yumna realised. *Waiting for it.*

'I dunno . . . a month?'

Kareem was grinning. 'It's happening. It's happening!' He clapped his hands once, twice, as if witnessing a gymnast land a particularly difficult routine. Nafisa let out a laugh, running over to Sadeeqa and enveloping her in a huge hug.

Even Sami nodded at Sadeeqa and offered a small smile.

'Welcome,' he said. 'Congratulations.'

'What . . . is going . . . on?' Sadeeqa muttered, staring at Yumna over Nafisa's shoulder. Yumna shrugged, at a loss. This was not at all what she expected. Nafisa had barely let go of Sadeeqa when they three began peppering her with queries.

'What are they saying, the voices?'

'When do you hear them? Are they all the same, or do they sound different?'

'Do you talk back?'

'Tell us everything!'

The questions flew from the lips of the older teens, and Sadeeqa faltered. Yumna could see her friend was becoming overwhelmed, her hands creeping up to her ears. She waded in and enveloped Sadeeqa in a side hug, putting her arm out like a bodyguard.

'*Enough!*' she snapped.

The bookshop fell silent.

'One at a time, OK? She's clearly fragile.'

The trio nodded, chastened. Everyone waited for Sadeeqa to speak. Slowly, she removed the sunglasses from her face. Her eyes were still all white.

'Right now, there's only a couple of voices.' Her voice was soft, uncertain. 'One is talking about being hungry, about how long it has been since it's eaten.' A pause. 'The other sounds like it's munching.' Sadeeqa straightened up now, and she sounded surer of herself.

'I don't hear them all the time, just when I'm not paying attention. Or sometimes, when I'm *really* paying attention. Whenever I start to hear them, this happens to my eyes.' She gestured at her face. 'I can't control it, it just happens.' On these last words, Yumna heard the quiver in her friend's voice, and reached for her hand, squeezing it. 'I don't think I can talk back. But I haven't tried.'

Sami looked pensive. 'I was scared at the beginning too,' he whispered. 'It's . . . intense.'

'You've got the same thing?' Sadeeqa's head turned to look at him. She couldn't hide her disappointment when Sami shook his head.

'Ah, no,' he said, his Midlands accent strong on the vowels. 'But you know, the change – it takes us all by surprise.'

'The Change?' Yumna hadn't heard of the phrase before, but it sounded important, like it would be written in ALL CAPS.

Nafisa kneeled down, gently taking Sadeeqa's hand into hers.

'You're going through what all of us have been through . . .'

Yumna held her breath. This was it! Finally, they were

going to get answers.

Ting-a-ling!

The front entrance bell rung, and they all turned.

'Am I interrupting?'

It was Hector.

CHAPTER NINE

Hector's presence changed everything. Nafisa busied herself with the new customer, transforming into the perfect bookseller in a blink. Yumna watched with trepidation, recalling her father's warning.

Stay away from the Maidstones . . .

Kareem quietly cleared his throat, stepping forward and indicating with his head for Sadeeqa to follow. Shoulders slumping, she followed him into the 'Translated Fiction' aisle, which Yumna knew was one of the least visited in the shop. It would be extremely dusty, a sneeze threatening every word of conversation.

Sami followed Kareem and Sadeeqa down Sneeze Alley, but when Yumna fell into step behind him, he turned and shook his head.

'I'm sorry,' he mouthed. 'Just Sadeeqa.'

Yumna stopped in her tracks, smarting, despite Sami's gentle dismissal. Why wasn't she allowed to join? Sadeeqa wouldn't even be having this conversation if Yumna hadn't dragged her here. *This was so unfair.* She considered following Sami anyway, but decided against it. If they wanted to keep secrets from her, fine. She'd just ask Sadeeqa to tell her everything later.

Yumna left the bookshop, glum. Nafisa and Hector were in such deep conversation when she had walked past them, they'd barely registered her presence. Her cousin did not even respond to her *salams* as she left. *Honestly*. What could be more important than wishing peace on a family member? She huffed and puffed, letting her annoyance be known, as she stomped down Whitby Street. She was so caught up in her thoughts, she did not notice Mrs Hardy waving from the BnB.

'Yoohoo!' Mrs Hardy called, for the third time. Only then did Yumna stop. *Eek!* She didn't want to speak to nosy Mrs Hardy, but once she'd had set her sights on you there was no getting out of it. The only thing worse than stopping to speak to Mrs Hardy was *not* stopping to speak to Mrs Hardy. The woman had a talent for spinning a tale.

'How is everything?' Mrs Hardy asked, as Yumna shuffled

up the perfectly paved front path. The BnB was her pride and joy, even more so than the choir. Its garden was in constant bloom, the beige brickwork covered in thick, climbable ivy, never a single blade of grass out of place. Yumna had once seen Mrs Hardy on her literal hands and knees, clipping the lawn with a tiny pair of scissors. Rumour was she was in the running for a national BnB award, but Yumna wasn't sure if the rumour was legit, or one Mrs Hardy started herself.

The proud proprietor was dressed as she always was, plain white button-up and light green trousers, covered by a flowery pastel apron tied at the waist. There was a dusting of flour across her chest, and a couple of grey hairs had escaped the bun, but all in all, she looked the picture of a perfect village BnB hostess. Yumna wondered if her own mother had been the type to wear an apron.

'Your friend Sadeeqa tell you about Nationals?' Mrs Hardy asked.

Ah, so this is about Sadeeqa.

'Oh, she mentioned something,' Yumna replied, looking down at her shoes to avoid Mrs Hardy's inquisitive gaze. Yumna didn't trust herself around the woman. She could pull secrets out of a fossil.

'Right. Yes, it is excellent news, is it not? She's a fantastic athlete, she really is. I always knew she would go to the international level. I tell you, I always saw it in her.' Yumna was sure two years ago Mrs Hardy was proclaiming Sadeeqa's career finished due to a small injury, but she was known for rewriting history to suit her. She clasped her hands together. 'Tell me, what do you know about the Maidstones?'

When Yumna mumbled something about not really talking to them yet, Mrs Hardy looked past her and down the street. 'Oh, I thought I saw Hector Maidstone walk into the bookshop a few minutes ago.'

She was good, Yumna thought. An annoying neighbour, but her skills of observation would make her an excellent private investigator.

'What was that?' Mrs Hardy asked, her tone suddenly sharp. 'Did you say something about a private investigator?'

'Nothing, sorry!' Yumna *really* needed to work on keeping her internal thoughts inside. Very un-detective-like behaviour. 'Yes, he did come into the shop,' she hurried on, keen to pretend the slip-up didn't happen. 'But he got talking to Nafisa straight away, I couldn't get a word in . . .'

A smile crept wolfishly across Mrs Hardy's face.

Oh gosh. Have I given away too much . . . ?

'Well. That's very good,' she said.

Is it? Yumna scratched her scalp through the jersey

fabric of her hijab. There was too much going on right now.

'Look at that.' The village gossip pointed down the road. A note of curiosity rang through her voice. 'Looks like the bookshop is very busy this afternoon . . .'

Yumna turned to see Sadeeqa walk out of the store, followed by Kareem, and Sami. *Right!*

'I've got to go, sorry!' She scurried back down the path and made a beeline for her friend. It was time she got some answers.

'Who's that young gentleman with them? Yumna? Oh, Yumna!'

'Sorry, Mrs Hardy! I'll see you later!'

Yumna didn't get a word out of her friend until the evening. Sadeeqa said nothing the whole walk home, and as soon as they were back in the house, started doing chores like her life depended on it. She also kept her sunglasses on all day, despite her siblings' jibes. While she seemed much calmer than she had in the morning, it was clear to Yumna not all Sadeeqa's questions had been answered.

'They said they would tell me everything tonight,' Sadeeqa admitted. The friends were ending the day as they had begun, crumpled up in the far corner of the bunk bed. 'But only if I go and meet them in the woods.'

Yumna's eyes widened. 'What? Why?'

Sadeeqa shrugged. 'I dunno.'

Yumna frowned. 'OK, well, I suppose I can sneak out again, or tell my dad I'm sleeping over at yours . . .'

Sadeeqa didn't reply, avoiding Yumna's gaze. A silence fell between them. Yumna could tell there was something else, something Sadeeqa didn't want to say. She waited patiently, watching the muscles in her friend's throat move as she swallowed, then spoke.

'They said I have to come alone.' Sadeeqa looked at Yumna guiltily.

'Oh.' Yumna tried to ignore the burning sensation blooming across her chest and face. She was grateful her skin was dark enough to hide her embarrassed blush. 'You're not going to listen to them, are you? We're best friends, we're—' She stopped speaking as Sadeeqa shook her head.

'They really meant it, Yumna.'

Yumna pushed herself backwards on the mattress, putting distance between Sadeeqa and herself. She didn't want to believe it. Surely, this was a joke!

'Since when do you listen to Kareem? This morning you were ready to rip his head off!'

'I need to know what's going on with me, Yumna!' Sadeeqa's reply was both petulant and apologetic. She felt bad, Yumna could tell. But not bad enough to change her mind.

'It's not fair!'

'I know. But you're not the one hearing voices in your head.' Sadeeqa turned away, facing the wall.

Yumna spluttered, finding herself unable to speak. After a few long seconds of confused stammering, she closed her mouth. Clearly, she had been dismissed.

Fine. If they want to be like that, she could play that game too.

Yumna left the room, left the house, and not once did she look back.

She would follow them, Yumna decided. She and Sadeeqa had done it once before. Well, now she would do it again, alone. She would pack her bag with all her equipment, sneak out in the middle of the night, and get close enough to hear their conversation. If they didn't want to let her in on the secret, she would have to find the secret out herself. What right did they have to hide things from her anyway? She was part of their group as much as anyone else!

Sadeeqa and Nafisa wouldn't have even become friends if it weren't for her. Sure, they might have met in the bookshop or at choir or Taekwondo, but that wasn't the point. The point was that she didn't want to be left out, as she always was. She was left out of having a mum, having siblings, getting her period. She wouldn't let this – whatever 'this' was – be another thing she wasn't a part of.

Yumna crept towards the edge of the tree line, doing her utmost not to make a sound. It was a warm night and the moon was out, shining like a dim searchlight over the woods. She had left her bag on a flat rock a few steps behind her, not wanting the large rucksack to accidentally snap a branch and blow her cover. But, given how engrossed in conversation the huddled teenagers looked, she needn't have bothered. She could jump up and down on the spot and the gathering around the fire wouldn't notice a thing. They might've been mere metres away, but they were in a world of their own.

Yumna wished she had ear binoculars to help eavesdrop; only snatches were audible over the cackling of the fire. She concentrated on their body language and tried to read their lips.

From what she could glean, it looked like Kareem was saying he was the 'first one', but the first one to do what? She couldn't tell. Then, Sami was nodding, gesturing at the fire, then—

A ball of flame burst out of his palm!

Yumna covered her mouth before any sound escaped. Sadeeqa jumped backwards too, shouting, but Sami looked serenely calm, especially for someone who had just produced a fireball out of thin air. His gaze was locked in on his palms, the glowing red heat flickering and dancing around his light brown skin. It was a ball the size of a marble, and from what Yumna could tell, it was a ball of pure *fire.* A few seconds later, he flicked his palm, once, twice, as if shaking off droplets of water.

Yumna watched, entranced, as the ball flew up into the sky. With his finger, Sami directed its movements, making it dance in the air, its bright core leaving a trail behind like a sparkler. *It was beautiful.*

After a few minutes, Sami brought it back to his palm, closed his fingers around the flame like it was a precious pearl and snuffed it out. He looked at Sadeeqa with a timid smile.

'I think I can actually *turn into* fire, but I've not been able to figure out how to do that yet.'

Yumna couldn't believe her eyes. How was this possible? Was it just a fancy trick? A hologram, or some new tech?

Sadeeqa must have thought the same thing, because suddenly she was stepping towards the fire, moving her hand into the flames.

'Oi!' Kareem barked. He pulled his sister back from the edge. 'You'll burn yourself!'

Sadeeqa grumbled, but did look chagrined. Yumna guessed that she'd gotten close enough to feel some real heat. *So, not a hologram*, Yumna thought. She needed to know more.

She furrowed her eyebrows and closed her eyes. *Focus on their voices.*

Slowly, she tuned out the sounds of the woods, the crackling of the fire, the light breeze through the trees. From her concealed position, as close as she could possibly be to the three teenagers without being seen, concentrating with all her might, Yumna could finally make out what they were saying.

'They're powers,' Kareem said. 'It's like magic.'

Sadeeqa was shaking her head. 'But we're Muslim, we don't believe in magic . . .'

Nafisa shrugged. 'We're not meant to use black magic, yeh. But that doesn't mean we don't believe in it. Also, this isn't black magic, this is different. I'm not cursing anyone. I just woke up one day and I could hear a bird at my window, yelling at me to let it in! Honestly, pigeons are so demanding. They're like the football hooligans of birds.'

Sami chuckled, despite himself.

'And what's my . . . power?' Sadeeqa asked, not looking very convinced.

'Sounds like you can talk to insects.'

Sadeeqa shook her head, staring into the fire. 'But why can't I hear anything now?'

Kareem shrugged. 'We're figuring out ways to control our abilities, but it's all kinda unpredictable.'

'What can you do?' Sadeeqa asked her brother. 'Are you also able to talk to animals?'

Kareem smiled. 'It's easier if I show you. You ready to have your mind blown?'

He closed his eyes and took a deep breath. The forest around them seemed to quieten, as if all the creatures in the woods were preparing to watch the performance.

Kareem took a step backwards, then another, and another. He paused, leaning forward, then took a step forward, focused and determined, a diver charging down a springboard, about to launch into the air. He was running towards the fire. Was he going to jump *into it*?

Then, mid-air, Kareem disappeared.

Sadeeqa cried out, her eyes wild, her feet skittering back and forth on the spot as she tried to understand what had just happened. Yumna blinked, wondering if her eyes were simply deceiving her. *Did Kareem just* disappear *into thin air?*

'Where the hell did he go?!' Sadeeqa was in full on panic mode now. Nafisa smiled, kindly.

'Just wait, sis. Just wait.'

A moment later, from the opposite end of the clearing

to where Yumna was crouching, in strode a glorious, golden horse. The same one that had jumped right over them a few nights earlier.

Yumna let out an audible gasp, at the same time as Sadeeqa.

Was that Kareem?!

As if she'd heard her, Sadeeqa whirled around, looking right at Yumna's hiding spot.

She wasn't sure if she'd been seen, but she didn't want to take any chances. Yumna turned, stumbled towards her backpack, and ran.

CHAPTER TEN

Once again, Yumna found herself alone in the fields.

It was not as dark this time, the clear night sky allowing the moon to do its thing. Yumna felt a bit like the moon tonight. She was important, and had her place, but the sun would always get the credit. Nafisa was the sun. *At least people write poems about the moon.* She couldn't think of any right now, but she knew they existed.

Mumbling quietly to herself, Yumna trudged on. The dark grass squeaked underneath her feet as she looked around, wondering if she would catch a glimpse of the monster she'd seen a few nights ago. It was easier to think of the Moonlight Monster than it was to process what she had just heard. Magic? Na-uh. It didn't make sense. There had to be some other explanation.

But there was no monster to be seen. All that was

visible were the massive round hay bales littered across the open field. For a moment, Yumna imagined the bales springing legs and waddling over to the barn when the humans weren't looking. Impossible, perhaps, but then, she'd just seen Sami make fire shoot out of his hands, so anything could happen . . .

Something dark moved behind a bale.

What was that? Yumna froze, then dropped to a crouch, holding still. If the bale *actually* sprouted legs and started to walk, she would start to think she was losing her mind.

Holding her breath so as not to make a sound, Yumna focused on where she had seen the movement.

There it was again!

The creature was tall, all black, and gleaming in the moonlight. It was standing still, apparently staring at the ground, then bent over and began to poke at the grass. *What on earth was it doing?*

A chill ran down Yumna's spine. She thought of Sami, plunging his hand into the fire, of Kareem, disappearing into thin air, then reappearing as a horse. If her eyes weren't deceiving her, that really *was* magic. If magic was real, then were monsters real too?

And if they were, one of them was standing less than a hundred metres away from her. Yumna didn't know whether to laugh or cry. What on earth was she meant to do?

Observe. That's all she could do, right? The voice of Mr Turner echoed in her ears. *Pay attention to what they do, not what they say.* He was talking about the Maidstones, yes, but Yumna felt confident that it could be applied here too.

She settled into her crouch, adjusting her weight and reaching for the binoculars hanging from a strap around her neck. She raised them to her eyes and sent a silent prayer of thanks for the help of the moonlight.

Up close, the Moonlight Monster looked . . . *curious.* Its face was a flat, blank surface, with two reflective globes for eyes, the size of golf balls. Its skin was baggy, it had mesh-like ears, and it moved like a toddler, or a giant bear – unsteady on two feet, but determined to keep moving forward. It waddled with its weight too far forward, as if its head was too heavy for its body. *What a strange creature.*

Yumna wondered what sort of magical power it possessed. Perhaps it spat poison, or could transform materials, or raise the dead? Maybe that's why it kept poking and prodding at the earth. *It looks like it is searching for something.*

She watched the Moonlight Monster comb the ground, walking back and forth between hay bales, making strange noises. She couldn't make sense of its actions, but this was the longest she'd seen it for. She figured it was time she got some answers.

★

Yumna dropped the binoculars from her eyes and sighed.

She'd been watching the Moonlight Monster do its funny walk all across the fields for ages, trying all her observational tricks to work out what it was doing, but nothing made sense.

Worse still? Now, despite keeping a close eye on its movements, Yumna had lost sight of the creature. It had ducked behind a bale and simply not reappeared. *Great.* She pondered her next course of action.

She wanted to solve the mystery of the Moonlight Monster, and she wanted to do it now. She needed to salvage something from this mess of a night!

What did she have to go off?

Yumna looked around and spotted the trail of prints in the dew that the Moonlight Monster had left, zigzagging across the field. She traced the steps with her gaze, trying to figure out whether or not there was a discernible pattern. Apart from covering almost every inch of visible field, she couldn't deduce anything more.

Yumna turned towards the BnB. It was a long shot, but the last time she had seen it, the Moonlight Monster had appeared to enter the BnB. Maybe it would do so again?

A light flickered on in a bedroom on the second floor of the BnB.

Yumna tried to see who was inside. It was too far away. *Binoculars!*

She fiddled with the focus wheel as she raised the lenses to her eyes. *This is creepy*, she thought. Peeking into a stranger's room in the dead of night was not the height of detective work. But something told her the answers to her questions lay in that room.

A silhouette approached the window pane. The shape was the body of a regular-sized man . . . but it had the *head* of the Moonlight Monster! *Subhanallah.* Yumna's eyes strained, but the light behind the creature meant she couldn't see any details. Then, the blank face turned, and Yumna felt the hairs on the back of her neck rise. The glass eyes were *staring right at her.*

The creature drew the curtains shut with a snap.

Yumna let go of the breath she had been holding.

She was right.

The Moonlight Monster . . . was in the BnB.

Yumna ran towards the BnB, all thoughts of her friends forgotten. She had to warn Mrs Hardy, had to tell her the BnB guests were in danger. She raced through the fields, but soon found herself slowing down to a semi-respectable jog. The fields were rather large, and she was beginning to wheeze rather dramatically. *I might need to work on my stamina,* Yumna thought, *if I'm to become a proper detective.* But then, she was carrying a rucksack that was almost half of her weight. *That* was probably why she was out of breath, not her total lack of fitness. Right?

Yumna geared herself up to enter the BnB. It was late, yes, but this was an urgent matter. She raised her hand to the back door ready to knock, but before her knuckles made contact with the painted wood, she paused.

A fistful of doubt grabbed her around the throat.

What if she was wrong?

Yumna took a step backwards, mentally taking stock. She *did* see the Moonlight Monster go into the BnB last time, and she definitely saw something that looked like the Moonlight Monster close the curtains of the top room just now. But what if it wasn't the Moonlight Monster? What if it was just an elderly fellow who woke up in the middle of the night to use the toilet, and his face looked like that because he wore one of those hydrating Korean face masks? She could have it all wrong, and that would lead to quite the humiliation.

Yumna wanted to avoid any shame and embarrassment. She needed to, especially after last summer.

It had been a misunderstanding, she had tried to tell people. She was trying to hone her detective skills, do the right thing. She hadn't meant for things to pan out the way they did.

Yumna had been suspicious of Sadeeqa's mum for some

time. Auntie had started doing all these strange things: getting up in the middle of the night to go on long walks alone, making long and strange phone calls, having wild mood swings and constantly worrying about money. According to the internet and all her detective novels, these were the sorts of behaviours exhibited by a criminal who is afraid of being caught. So, like a good citizen detective, Yumna went into the village hall after market day, found the man with the shiniest buttons and most number of chevrons on his uniform, and told him she had something important to say. She told the policeman Sadeeqa's mum was hiding a secret, something major and something important, and he simply *had* to come and see.

It turned out that Auntie was pregnant.

Yes, this was major and important, the policeman had told her with a chuckle, but it was not a police matter.

Yumna had not been able to live that down. Indeed, it had been the talk of the village for months. It was a miracle – a genuine miracle – that Sadeeqa and her mother had forgiven her, and that people weren't still laughing at her whenever she walked past. It wasn't entirely her fault, Yumna felt. She didn't know anything about babies, she had no siblings and no mother around, so how was she supposed to know the signs? Ultimately yes, no crime had been committed, but, Yumna maintained, she was right about there being a secret!

She hadn't gotten any credit for that.

That was last summer.

This summer would be different. She had promised herself that.

Yumna took a deep breath and lifted her hand again. She knew what she had seen. She was sure of it. She was going to tell Mrs Hardy.

But just as she was about to knock, the door swung open.

The light from inside the lobby blinded her, momentarily.

All she heard was a deep voice, gravelly and harsh.

'Can I help you?'

As her eyes adjusted, Yumna's insides ran cold.

It was the creature from the upstairs bedroom!

Yumna opened her mouth, but she was too stunned to speak. She squinted, trying to better see the creature who spoke.

'Why don't you come inside?' the deep voice said. To Yumna's surprise, it didn't sound scary. In fact, if she wasn't mistaken, the creature sounded almost nervous.

Monsters don't have feelings . . . do they?

'I'm here to see Mrs Hardy,' Yumna managed to stutter out, averting her eyes. She had realised at the last minute that perhaps this monster had the power of Medusa. What if making eye contact with its glass eyeballs would turn her into stone, or sludge, or something? She had to keep all her wits about her.

'She won't be awake for hours.' A pause. 'Are you lost, little one?'

Yumna blinked in confusion. Why was this monster being nice to her? Was this some sort of ploy to lure her into the house before stripping the flesh from her bones?

'Come inside now,' the creature rasped, stepping over the threshold and reaching out. She jerked her body out of reach, but the momentum forced her to stumble and trip over the uneven ground. She fell backwards, landing with a thud on her rucksack, her arms and legs sticking out in the air like an upturned turtle.

Yumna stared up at the sky. She couldn't see any stars, but the pale disc of the moon seemed to wink at her as a light grey cloud drifted across its face. She could hear the crunch of gravel as the creature made its way towards her.

Crunch, crunch, crunch.

She could hear her heart pounding in her ears as she struggled to get up. It was no use. The weight of the backpack was too heavy, she realised. She had overpacked, and now, those emergency provisions were going to be the death of her.

Yumna squeezed her eyes shut, whispering the shahada

under her breath. If she was going to die, she wanted these to be the last words she ever said. *I believe there is no god but Allah, and the Prophet Mohammed is Allah's messenger. I believe there's no god but Allah . . .*

Yumna felt two strong hands grip the tops of her arms and haul her to her feet.

This was it.

This was the end.

Yumna blacked out.

CHAPTER ELEVEN

When Yumna came round, she was seated upright in a soft leather armchair, facing a soothing fire. The room was dimly lit, cosy and familiar. She stretched, yawning as she woke up, before the moments preceding her fainting spell came rushing back to her with the speed of an oncoming train. She sat bolt upright, then waved her arms to make sure she wasn't tied to the armchair like some sort of prisoner.

'Where am I?' she asked aloud. 'Hello, is anyone there?'

'Hey, hey, no need to yell. I'm right here.'

The voice came from the sofa to her right. Taking in the colonial-style paintings hanging from the walls and ceramic pottery of dogs crowding the mantelpiece, Yumna realised she was in the lounge area of the BnB. With horror, she saw the voice belonged to none other than the *Moonlight Monster*, and it was sitting *right next to her in this very room!*

From up close, she could smell it. Fresh soil and old sweat. She fumbled for the torch in her breast pocket, pulling it out and shining it right into the creature's face. Finally, finally, she would see this terrifying abomination in all its horrific, scary glory.

The creature groaned in discomfort.

'What— What are you doing?'

Yumna stared, wondering whether she could trust her eyes. She waved the torch up and down, turning its beam away, then bringing it back. She couldn't believe it.

The creature sitting on the sofa wasn't a monster. It was just a regular-looking, slightly pale, human man.

'Where's—' Yumna stammered. 'Where did it go? It was just— I swear . . .'

The man was a lean fellow, long and sinewed like someone who spent a lot of time outdoors rock climbing, or setting up tents. Yumna guessed he was the type of person who enjoyed a walking holiday, ate granola and lived in hiking boots. He wore thick glasses, had brown, floppy hair that he kept pushing out of his eyes, and ears large enough to double as satellite dishes.

He looked nothing like the Moonlight Monster.

Where had it gone?

She knew she hadn't imagined it. Maybe it had transformed into this man while she was out cold!

'Do you mind?' the man said, waving his hand at the torch. 'I'm sorry, it's hurting my eyes.'

He sounded Scottish, but accents were not Yumna's strong suit. She lowered the light and slipped the torch back into her pocket.

'You should have something to drink.' He nodded at the two mugs he had set on the coffee table in front of her. 'I wasn't sure what you might want, so we have some peppermint tea and hot chocolate. I hope cow's milk is fine? I can also send for some water or another drink if you'd prefer, Mrs Hardy is likely awake now.'

Yumna let out a scoff.

'Is there poison in them? Is that what this is? Are you going to poison me and then eat me alive? What kind of monster are you?'

Yumna was attempting to channel the tough, cool demeanour of her favourite fictional detectives. It wasn't quite having the desired effect.

The man looked shocked for a moment, then a look of understanding slowly dawned across his face.

'Ohhh . . .' he said, before getting up and leaving the room.

When the man returned, he was half monster, half human. From the waist down, it was the body of the Hulk, with black, shiny skin. From the waist up, he was a regular nerdy guy.

'I'm sorry to have frightened you, lassie. It's just my boiler suit.'

She took in the sight at close range.

'I'm Norton, by the way. Pleasure to make your acquaintance.'

So, the scary creature was just this innocent-looking man in a costume?

Yumna couldn't help but feel tricked. '*You're* the Moonlight Monster?'

He chuckled, shuffling over to the sofa and lowering his weight on to the cushion with obvious effort. He heaved a large item from under his arm on to the coffee table. Yumna recognised the blank expression and glass eyeballs of the Moonlight Monster's face. *This was the mask she had seen in the window!*

'That's one way to put it, I s'pose.'

'What's going on? Who are you? Why have you been sneaking around in the fields in the middle of the night, wearing *that* –' Yumna pointed at the helmet – 'on your head?'

The man smiled.

'You know . . . I've been doing this for years now, but you're the only one who's ever spotted me.' He raised his eyebrows. 'You're a clever girl, anyone ever told you that?'

Yumna tried not to let the flattery get to her, but she

couldn't resist a small grin.

'I have been known for my powers of observation,' she replied, choosing to ignore the times when those powers were wildly off.

'Aye, I can believe that.'

The silence was filled with soft crackling from the fireplace. Yumna resisted the urge to jump in with questions. Something about this man's energy – slow and steady on the surface but with an undercurrent of nervous intensity – made her think she would have more success waiting for him to speak first.

She took a sip of the hot chocolate, nodding with approval at its thick texture. This was a man who knew how to make a tasty hot chocolate! But when had he had the time? Had she been knocked out for that long?

'Have you ever heard of a herpetologist?' When he spoke, it was almost a shock. She had gotten used to the quiet. Yumna shook her head.

'Aye. I hadn't heard of one either when I was about your age. But I was always one.' He tapped his chest. 'Here. In my heart.'

The man leaned back into the sofa, the leather creaking and groaning as he settled in. 'I always loved me some herpetofauna.'

'Her-what now?' It sounded like a disease.

'Herpetofauna. Reptiles and amphibians,' he clarified. 'Frogs, toads, newts, lizards, the lot. Anything a bit slimy or, in the scientific sense, any cold-blooded vertebrate tetrapod – four-legged creature with a spine – that's my remit.'

'So . . . you're trying to become a four-legged creature with a spine? Is that what this is all about?' Yumna snorted.

He laughed, from his belly this time, although he kept his voice low. 'No, no. I study them, you see. But,' he lowered his voice further, forcing Yumna to lean forward in order to hear him, 'I'm out here on a secret project. That's why the outfit.' He indicated the boiler suit, and the mask. 'To hide my identity, both from the newt, and from any spies . . .'

Yumna's jaw dropped. Actual *spies*?! In Silverbrook? Now they were talking.

Norton was nodding. 'Aye.'

'What's the secret project?'

Norton looked to his left and his right, as if to check the spy wasn't sitting right beside him in the BnB. 'If I tell you, I'll have to kill you . . .'

Yumna's eyes bulged from their sockets. Norton's expression turned from serious to boyish, in a flash.

'I'm only joking. I can tell you, but only because I've finished the project. Tonight was my last night on the job.'

He beamed. 'Tell me, lassie. Do you know who owns all the land behind this BnB?'

'The fields, you mean?' Yumna shook her head. She hadn't ever given much thought to who owned the farmlands. She preferred looking at the houses; she knew who owned all of those. But open fields? Who cares?

'Yes, the fields. You see, many of them are owned by whoever lives up in Wenning Keep, and they have historically paid people to do the farming.'

Yumna thought of her father, who worked long hours every day on other people's farms. She supposed her father was only one of the people the castle people paid to do the work they didn't want to do.

'But the new family, the Maidstones, they've now inherited the estate, and all the land that comes with it.'

The Maidstones. For a family that had only just moved into the neighbourhood, Yumna was hearing quite a lot about them. They certainly had made a splash!

'But they're not so interested in farming, these Maidstones.'

'How come? What does it matter anyway, can't they just do what the old guy before did and pay someone to do the farming for them?'

Norton shook his head. 'They need a lot more money to renovate the building, so they're looking at other, better paying options. Can you guess what?'

Yumna hummed, trying to think. 'Digging for gold? Solar panels?' Though perhaps in cloudy Silverbrook, solar panels weren't a thing.

Norton laughed. 'Not quite. What makes a lot more money in a place like this is *commerce.*'

When Yumna's blank expression didn't change, he clarified. 'I mean, shops!'

'But we have shops?'

'Yes, but do you have a *supermarket*?'

Oh. My. Goodness.

A supermarket?! The nearest supermarket was three villages away, and Yumna only got to go there once a month, if she was lucky. Here in Silverbrook they were stuck with the village shop, which was fine, but was nothing like a Big Supermarket.

'The Maidstones want to build a supermarket?'

Norton nodded, conspiratorially. Yumna's jaw hit the floor.

'That's so exciting!' Yumna's voice rose again, but she dropped it at Norton's warning look. 'But what's that got to do with you?'

'Excellent question.'

Out of a hidden pocket in the Moonlight Monster boiler suit, Norton pulled out a model of a strange-looking creature.

'Do you know what this is?' Norton held up the model of the creature. It was a newt, but not like one Yumna had seen before. Its body was mostly dark brown, but its underbelly was a glorious mustardy colour, speckled with large black spots. On its spine was a sort of raised jagged ridge that travelled all the way down its back. From nose to tail, it fitted on Norton's palm.

'It's a model of a great crested newt,' Norton said, answering his own question. 'One of the rarest types of newts in the country. A protected species because it's declining in population. And wouldn't you know it . . . this little guy is native to this area.'

Norton handed the model to Yumna, who turned it over in her hands, inspecting it closely. It was quite beautiful, in an otherworldly kind of way.

'There had been reports of this newt being seen on the Maidstones' land. If I had found any, the development would have been halted before it could begin.'

The pieces were beginning to fall into place.

'Is this why it had to be secret?'

Norton nodded. 'That's right. So that no one could interfere with the newts, if any were around . . .'

'Did you find anything?'

Norton shook his head. 'Sadly, no sign of any great crested newts. Lots of other creepy-crawlies, but not the one that matters. Shame, though. Not sure this place needs a supermarket . . .' He paused. 'Oh, my!'

Norton had noticed the time on the wall clock.

'It's eleven o'clock, well past your bedtime. You need to get home, lassie. Come on.'

Yumna sighed as she let herself out of the BnB's back gate.

Well, that was the mystery of the Moonlight Monster solved.

She felt like she ought to be elated. She had single-handedly solved a mystery, without embarrassing herself in the process (not too much, anyway – the fainting didn't count). But Yumna had never expected that when she finally cracked the case, she would find herself all alone. She hadn't expected her two best friends to be on their own separate adventure without her. Sure, she'd had her own escapades, but they were much more fun when shared with friends, weren't they?

Yumna took one last look at the woods before she headed home.

What were they doing there? Did they all really have magic?

She exhaled loudly, feeling like she'd ended the night with more questions than she'd started. As she turned away from the tree line, another flicker of movement caught her eye.

Peering through her binoculars for the last time that night, Yumna spotted a figure snaking his way through the trees.

Was that Norton going back into the woods?

Probably searching for more rare newts, she thought, dropping the lenses. A heavy melancholy settled on Yumna as she trudged home. What was the point? Of going on adventures, of solving mysteries, if she was always going to be alone?

CHAPTER TWELVE

Yumna didn't say a word when she crept back into the house and found her father sitting at the kitchen counter, his worried face in his hands. Not when he scolded her for sneaking out in the middle of the night for the second time that week, threatening to ground her for the rest of the summer if he caught her out late again. What was she doing out in the woods anyway? Didn't she know the world could be dangerous for young girls?

She didn't say a word when Mr Gareth called, wondering why she hadn't gone out for the paper round the next morning. There had been complaints. Didn't she know that reliability was the most important quality of a paper-person? A newspaper was only useful on the day it was printed, the boss reminded her, but still Yumna said nothing.

Yumna stayed quiet from dawn till dusk, and deep into

the next night. Despite the summer warmth, she buried herself under her duvet, wiping away the sweat dampening her pyjamas, ignoring the notifications pinging on her phone.

This wasn't how it was meant to be. By the time she'd made it home, the adrenaline of the night had worn off, and the gravity of the night's events began to sink in. She'd solved the mystery of the Moonlight Monster, but instead of celebrating, she was hiding away. All her friends were hanging out without her. They had flipping *magical powers* and what did she have? Absolutely nothing! Some story about a man who wore a shiny black baggy suit and wandered around in the middle of the night looking for rare newts, of all things. Not even searching for something exciting, like dinosaur bones or an ancient crown or diamonds. Just little speckled amphibians that were endangered in this world. What a disappointment. A rare newt was no competition for turning into a GOLDEN HORSE!

Under her duvet, Yumna closed her eyes and tried to focus her senses. Maybe she did have powers, but they just hadn't kicked in yet? She reached out with her mind, trying to connect with the trees outside – *wouldn't it be cool if she could talk to plants?* – but all she could feel was the scratch of fabric against her skin, all she could hear were her own thoughts, rattling around like loose marbles in her head. No luck there.

Later, when the house was quiet and she was sure her father had fallen asleep, Yumna padded to the bathroom and filled up the sink. Eyeing the warm water with intention, she muttered *Bismillah*, and dunked her face under the surface, stopping just short of her hairline. After a moment, she tried to take a deep breath in. The water shot up her nostrils and she reeled back, pulling her head out of the sink, choking and gagging, wiping the water away from her eyes. Looks like she couldn't breathe under water, either.

After sticking her hand above a candle, imagining herself transforming into various creatures and even trying to enter a different dimension through the back of her cupboard, Yumna gave up on trying to discover her hidden magic.

I don't even want powers, Yumna tried to convince herself. She'd never been the type of kid who imagined herself a superhero, able to save the world if she could just turn invisible. No, it wasn't the powers she was sad about (though she wouldn't say *no* to having magical powers, either, if she was given the option). It was more that everyone else seemed to have them except her. What was that about? Why did everyone else get to be special?

Did it have something to do with her mum?

The thought bothered Yumna, but then it got her thinking. Did the adults know about the powers?

Yumna highly doubted it. If Nafisa's parents knew their

daughter had developed the ability to communicate with birds, they would have packed her off to magic school already. They were big on maximising Nafisa's potential, and this definitely fell under the category of 'a skill one should maximise'. Yumna wasn't sure magic schools even existed outside of fantasy books though, so maybe they would have sent her to the local vet instead, to make the best use of her bird-communication ability.

What was it like, understanding animals? Were they more interesting than humans? Did they have opinions? Were there some animals or birds that were more well-spoken than others? Did they have different interests?

She imagined that owls sounded grand and wise, while sparrows had high-pitched, gossipy voices. Owls would watch *Antiques Roadshow*, and sparrows *Real Housewives of Atlanta*. She wondered if the birds felt like they were ever stereotyped or misunderstood. Was there a little robin that felt like it had the soul of an eagle, or a hummingbird who hated singing? Were hawks ever tired of being so predatory? Did they ever want to just put their feet up, and have someone else bring them dinner? Was there a vulture that wanted to be vegetarian?

Yumna was bursting with questions. Like, Sadeeqa could communicate with insects. Did that mean all of them? Could she talk to them all together, or could she only talk to them one by one? Did each insect speak a different language, or did they just have dialects? She wondered if different creatures had different accents, like whether the ants from Liverpool sounded like the ants from Aberdeen.

Oh, she had so many things to ask. But she wasn't going to beg. If they didn't want to invite her into their magical world, she would have to settle for not knowing any of the answers and hang out in bed, by herself, alone with her thoughts.

'Yumna?'

Her father knocked once on the door and entered the room. It was early, Yumna guessed he had just prayed Fajr. Her father looked tired but determined. 'Come on, you've been in bed for days. Khalas, you're not sick, I know you're not. It's time to stop sulking. Get up and go outside!'

He pulled up the blinds with a snap and pushed open the window. It was a clear morning, the sky rudely blue and cheerful, a stark contrast to the doom and gloom inside Yumna's bedroom.

'It stinks in here, Yumna. What have you been doing?'

Yumna had been doing nothing, that was the problem. After she'd given up on uncovering her non-existent powers, she'd fallen into a stupor, sulking and feeling sorry for herself. At some point, she had even switched her phone *off, completely,* an unprecedented action for a teenage girl, but a very effective way to ignore the world.

'Come look,' her father said, beckoning her over to the window.

She dragged herself reluctantly and was surprised to see Sadeeqa jumping up and down trying to get her attention, and Nafisa beside her, arms crossed and slouching. Even though she was trying to ignore it, the outside world was not ready to forget her just yet.

'Why don't you want to see your friends? The girls have been coming by the house every morning this week, I can't keep turning them away.' The furrow between her father's eyes deepened. 'Is everything OK? Is it . . .' He coughed awkwardly, bending down to perch on the edge of her bed. 'You know . . . *that* time of the month?'

'Baba!' She couldn't believe that now *her* father was trying to talk to her about periods. So gross. She had nothing to report on that front anyway.

'You can talk to me about anything, Yumna, you know that?'

'Yes, Baba. But no, it's not . . . Nothing like that.' These were the first proper sentences she'd spoken in ages. Her voice was raspy from lack of use, but she still managed to sound sarcastic.

'Ah,' he said, sounding almost . . . disappointed?

He reached into the pocket of his dressing gown and pulled out a squashed cube-shaped package. Yumna recognised it immediately from the bright pink and florals and stifled a groan.

'I got you these, just in case.'

'Baba!'

Her father was handing her a packet of sanitary pads, as if it were the most normal thing in the world. Honestly, how awkward! Had anyone seen him buy them in the shops? They would know the pads were for her. So embarrassing, especially because she still hadn't even started getting periods! Yumna wondered if her friends – her *former* friends – could see this exchange through the window, and pulled her duvet over her head in humiliation.

'Yumna, habibi.' Baba gently removed the duvet from her face. 'It's OK. There's nothing to be ashamed about, it's perfectly natural.'

'It's not though, is it.' Her voice had lost its barb now. It was just sad. He looked at his daughter with concern.

'What do you mean?'

Yumna shrugged, unable to meet his eyes. She knew what she was going to say would hurt him, but she couldn't change how she felt. She looked outside the window, where Sadeeqa and Nafisa were now sitting on the ground, scrolling on their phones.

'None of the other girls do this with their dads. They all have their mums to talk to about this stuff.' She remembered Mr Sulaiman's face as he'd mentioned trying to talk to Sadeeqa.

Yumna's father sighed, wrapping his daughter in a bear hug. 'That might be true, but I want you to know I'm here for you, Yumna – about this and about anything else.'

A tear slid down her face, unbidden.

'Why did she have to leave, Baba?' She pushed her father away, staring into his eyes, searching for the answer. 'Why wasn't I enough?'

'Oh, Yumna.' He shook his head and rubbed his face with his hands. He looked like he did every time they had this conversation. Utterly distraught. 'It wasn't your fault, you know that. I've told you that. She was leaving to protect you. It wasn't your fault.'

Yumna shrugged her shoulders, her pain morphing into anger. 'Protect me from what? You say it wasn't my fault, but then whose was it then? Was it yours? Was it something you did? How could leaving me be protecting me?' She could see her words hit her father like punches, wounding him with every blow, but she could not stop. It was not fair, none of this was fair. 'How can a mother walk out on her husband and daughter and never look back, never get in touch, nothing? It's like . . .' Yumna searched for the words that she had often thought but never dared to utter. 'It would have been easier if she'd died! At least that would make sense!'

'Enough!' he snapped. Yumna's father stood up and raised his hand, as if to defend himself from her barrage of insults. He looked broken, defeated, but rather than feeling sorry, Yumna felt . . . embarrassed? Ashamed? Disappointed? In that moment, she hated her father for his softness, his weakness. Why couldn't he just answer her questions?

'Don't speak about your mother like that.' He turned away from his daughter, but Yumna saw distress flash across his face before he covered it with a neutral expression. 'You don't know what you're saying.' He paused, inhaling deeply, then letting out his breath slowly before speaking again.

'Your words are more powerful than you realise, Yumna. Be careful with how you use them.'

With that, he left the room.

Yumna buried herself under her duvet once more. There was no way she was leaving the house today.

Hours later, Yumna decided to switch her phone back on. She was curious about what her friends had been up to.

As her phone loaded up, notifications tumbled in, one after the other, at a speed which made Yumna's head spin. *Well, at least she was popular!*

She wondered what all the fuss was about. Part of her hoped that maybe they had been missing her, and these were all the messages they had sent begging her to come hang out. Maybe they were sharing stories about their magical adventures, and felt that Yumna *had* to know, because she was a key part of the friendship group, right?

As she clicked through, Yumna noticed most of the notifications weren't private messages. In fact, none of them were. The group chat she had with Nafisa and Sadeeqa was conspicuously quiet. All the notifications had come from a newly created group chat, titled 'FINDING K'.

Huh?

She opened the group chat and sucked her breath in as she began to read.

Members of the chat were the 'magic circle', as she had decided to call them: Nafisa, Sadeeqa, Sami and Kareem.

Nobody had seen Kareem since Yumna had followed them into the woods. That was a few nights ago. From what she could tell, there had been a fight, and then Kareem had disappeared. Everyone assumed he would turn up that day, or even that night. But when Sadeeqa woke up this morning and he still hadn't slept in his bed, she had started to get worried. They had *all* started to get worried.

Yumna thought back to that morning. *So, this is what they were waving at the window about.*

It wasn't a wave of 'Hey, we miss you,' it was a wave of 'Hey, check your phone because my brother is missing'. A small, but important distinction.

'This is getting serious,' Sadeeqa had said in a voice note. 'My parents are asking questions now.'

Nafisa had replied almost instantly. 'Just tell them he's gone to the next village or something.'

But Yumna knew that wouldn't work. It was Friday, and Kareem never missed going to the mosque for Juma'a prayer with his father. If he had missed Friday prayers and hadn't called, or messaged, or turned up in the hospital then it was definitely time to start panicking.

'Hey, everyone . . .' she typed. 'I know I'm like, the only one without powers or whatever. But I do think it's time you tell the parents.'

She waited for the next notification to pop up. She watched Nafisa *typing*, three dots glowing tantalisingly on her screen.

Then, the dots were gone.

Sadeeqa began *typing*, then, she too stopped before a message came through. Yumna couldn't handle the tension.

Hello . . . she typed. Anyone?

Once again, the chat fell silent.

Then a message popped up, from Nafisa. Sorry, cuz.

Next thing: *Yumna has been removed from the group chat.*

?!

She threw her phone on the duvet. She *hated* this! Why was this happening?

Yumna raised her face to the ceiling and begged God to explain.

Ya Allah, why?!

CHAPTER THIRTEEN

At choir that afternoon, Yumna couldn't hide her disbelief. *They're pretending nothing's happened.*

She had swallowed her pride and dragged herself out of the house, much to her father's delight. Once in Shington Hall, she attempted to bring up the group chat situation with her cousin, but Nafisa had pretended she didn't know what Yumna was talking about. Sadeeqa, wearing her sunglasses inside again, was ignoring Yumna completely. Was Kareem even still missing? She had no idea.

Yumna had tried sitting next to them in the front row, but since she was not a soprano, she'd been moved back to her usual spot by Mrs Hardy. Now, she was sitting next to the retired doctors, who had both been sucking on boiled sweets and did not involve her in their conversation.

This sucks.

'Everyone!' Mrs Hardy clapped her hands, demanding the choir's attention. The hubbub in the room subsided as the singers turned to face their conductor.

'I have some news,' Mrs Hardy said. She was so full of excitable energy, she couldn't stand still. Yumna wondered what news could possibly make her so happy – she didn't even remember Mrs Hardy being this excited when her daughter gave birth to twins, and everyone knows twins are the best surprise. Two for the price of one! The only thing better, Yumna figured, was triplets.

'You are all aware that the monthly market is happening this weekend right here in Shington Hall.' Her smooth cheeks were glowing pink. 'Well, thanks to the kind initiative and sponsorship from our new villagers.' Mrs Hardy raised her hand to point to Hector and Sybil, who had taken their respective seats among the choir, 'I am pleased to announce that the Silverbrook Choral Group has been invited to perform!' She clapped her hands and beamed. 'Isn't that spectacular?'

A wave of surprise and anticipation rumbled through the choir. Yumna looked to her left, making eye contact with the retired doctor beside her. 'My, my,' he said, but that was it. There was no one sitting to Yumna's right, so no one she could share her reaction with. Peering over to the front row, she tried to get a glimpse of how Sadeeqa and Nafisa were responding, but she couldn't see over everyone's heads. She was the shortest in the group, after all.

While there was no doubt this was a huge opportunity for the whole choir, it was the biggest deal for Nafisa, who would have numerous solos in any group outing. She might get spotted by a talent scout, maybe even go viral online. The right mix of ingredients and this kind of thing could change Nafisa's life.

Despite her annoyance, Yumna sent up a little prayer. *Ya Allah, please bless this opportunity for Nafisa. Make it easy for her to share her gift with the world.*

The prayer did make Yumna wonder what *her* gift to share with the world could be. It definitely wasn't magical.

'Depending on how we go this weekend, the committee has even said that there could be opportunity to *travel* with the market!'

Someone gasped.

'That's right,' Mrs Hardy smiled. 'We have the potential to tour with our performances, not only wowing audiences across the county, but using it to practise for the big competition in autumn.'

'We could make quite a name for ourselves,' whispered one of the elderly doctors. 'With the young lass's talent,' his partner said, nodding in Nafisa's direction, 'we might even make the local radio! My bridge group will be so jealous.'

'This is all the wonderful work of Hector and Sybil,' Mrs Hardy beamed, and the choir duly applauded.

At this, Hector rose from his seat, doing up the button of his jacket. *He wears a jacket to choir?* Honestly, these Maidstones were out of an eighteenth-century novel. Yumna unlocked her phone to send the girls a joke, remembering halfway through typing that they weren't talking. *Damn.* It hurt, every time.

'Thank you for your kind words, Mrs Hardy,' Hector began. Once again, Yumna thought he exuded the energy of the unassuming man in a back corner of a popular restaurant who actually owned every building on the street. Landlord energy. It was a combination of wealth, power and the sense that he knew he could get whatever he wanted. *Stay away from the Maidstones . . .* It occurred to Yumna that if you were on the right side of the Maidstones, you could fulfil your heart's desires – like the choir performance. She wondered if that changed when things *didn't* go their way. Had that ever happened? It seemed unlikely.

'The Chair of the committee has been a friend of mine for a long time, so it was a simple ask,' Hector continued, his voice mild. 'But as we said,' he smiled in Sybil's direction, 'we are thrilled to be a part of village life here in Silverbrook, so do let us know what else we can do.' He took his seat.

Why are the Maidstones being so nice?

Yumna decided not to return home straight after choir. Sadeeqa would be going the same way, and she couldn't handle the awkwardness of being on the same street but not walking together. She couldn't go down Eastbourne Lane, either, because that's where Nafisa lived. So, she headed down Whitby, waving a cheery goodbye in case anyone wondered why she was walking in the wrong direction. Her goodbye said, *I'm just going for a walk, don't worry, nothing's the matter*, but as she waved, she realised nobody had been paying attention to her in the first place.

That old invisibility strikes again.

She sighed.

Shoulders hunched, Yumna walked up Whitby Street and ran over the facts in her mind. She picked up each thought like a precious rock, turning it over and examining it closely, wondering if it would reveal anything new.

Her friends had magical powers. Weird, but OK. Nobody had explained why, or how they worked, but all of them – including her cousin – seemed to have them. They came on without warning, and all seemed somehow related to nature – fire, insects, birds, becoming a horse . . .

Then, there was the mystery of the Moonlight Monster. She had thought that maybe the creature would be connected to the magic powers, but it appeared to be more about the Maidstones wanting to make more money. *Classic.* That all seemed to be all sorted out now that she had met Norton the herpetologist, and he had revealed his hunt for the rare newt.

But then, what about Kareem going missing? She had seen Norton go into the forest the night Kareem disappeared, but were those things connected? Yumna couldn't be sure. What would a herpetologist want with a magical teenager? She couldn't decide whether this was another mystery she should try to solve, or some 'powers' thing she was going to be kept out of.

'Hello there!'

Yumna looked around her, trying to place the origin of the voice. It was still light, the sky streaked with a brilliant sunset of amber and gold. But the street was deserted, not a soul to be seen on the footpaths either side of the asphalt. Most of this stretch of Whitby Street was surrounded by high fences and oak trees, so it was unlikely someone had seen Yumna and was calling from their garden . . .

'Over here!'

Sitting out the front of the BnB, looking comfortable

on a metal garden chair, was none other than Norton. He was sitting on the first-floor balcony, with a view of the entire village.

'How was choir practice? You all sound very . . .' He searched for the word. 'In tune!'

Yumna grinned. At least here was one person who paid attention to her.

'You're not a monster today?'

Norton smiled. 'No, I've put the boiler suit away now. Will bring it out for Halloween though, I think.' He paused, closing the book in his hand slightly, a frown crossing his face as he looked at Yumna.

'Are you all right there? Why the long face?'

Yumna looked down at her feet. This was the downside of people paying attention. They noticed what was really going on.

'Hey, lassie. Don't be sad now.'

She looked back up, pasting a smile across her face. 'I'm fine.' When his facial expression remained worried, she doubled down. 'Really, I am. Thank you, though. For asking. Have a nice night, and good luck with the ne—'

She stopped herself from finishing the sentence when Norton's eyes bulged and he motioned for her not to mention the word 'newt'. *Oh yeah, it's a secret!*

Norton tapped his finger against the cover of his book,

then seemed to arrive at a decision. 'Wait there a moment, just one moment.'

Two minutes later, Norton was walking through the front door of the BnB, wearing his hiking boots and holding two walking sticks. A pair of binoculars swung from his neck. It was a serious bit of kit, Yumna noticed. She hadn't come across that brand before, its logo a glowing symbol that looked like a cross between a target and a lightning bolt. Maybe it was some sort of specialist equipment? Herpetologists must need the best.

Norton handed Yumna a book. It was thick, with a sketch of a countryside landscape on its front.

'*The Walker's Guide to Outdoor Clues & Signs*, by Tristan Gooley,' she read out loud.

'What's this?'

'The first-time hiker's bible,' Norton replied.

'The first-time hiker's Qur'an, you mean?' she teased.

Norton paused, then chuckled. 'Yes, exactly.' He looked out over the field behind the BnB, where the hay bales still lay like scattered game pieces across a board.

'We've only got about half an hour of good light left, but why don't we use it? Let's go see what the field has to offer.'

'The field? There's nothing in the fields!'

'That's where you would be wrong, miss. The natural world is full of wonders, but you have to know what you're looking for. You love detective books, don't you?' Yumna nodded, not stopping to wonder how he knew that. 'Well, think of walking through the fields as practising your nature-detective muscles, OK?'

Yumna bit her bottom lip, trying to decide what to do. He was a stranger, but a nice stranger, and if they stuck to the fields then she could easily find her way home if anything felt weird. She wondered what Sadeeqa and Nafisa would do in her place, then promptly dismissed the thought. They had dumped her! So she could do whatever she wanted. The question should be, *What would Yumna do!*

'OK, I'll come,' she decided. 'But only for half an hour. I need to get back before it's dark, or my dad will freak out and probably ground me.'

Norton raised his thumb to make the universal sign for *Of course!*

'Let me also just . . .'

Yumna pulled out her phone and clicked into the dormant group chat between Sadeeqa, Nafisa and herself. She dropped in her live location. 'I'm going for a walk with a herpetologist, FYI in case I disappear.'

She waited. Her messages were delivered, but not read.

She could see they were both online.

Fine.

'I'm ready!' she said to Norton. 'Let's go!'

CHAPTER FOURTEEN

As Yumna returned from an evening of nature exploration, she bumped into Mr Turner.

'You're back!' She rarely got to see Mr Turner at the end of the day.

He looked as well turned out as he did every morning, as if the day's exertions hadn't happened.

Mr Turner smiled warmly. 'The Maidstones have begun their renovations, so I've been given some much needed time off.'

Her eyes widened. 'Does that mean you get a holiday? What are you going to do? Another one of your long walks?'

Although Mr Turner was a butler, he was also known to be quite the explorer. Not only did he hike the *thousand* miles every morning to the Castle on the Hill (wearing his penguin outfit too, Yumna didn't know how he did it), but he had once walked, according to Mrs Hardy, all the way from Inverness in Scotland, to Southampton, in the south of England. It had taken Mr Turner six weeks and two pairs of shoes, apparently. Yumna had been shocked; she didn't even know walking that far was *possible*!

'How do you think people used to get to places back in the old days?' Mr Turner had said when she'd asked. Yumna had simply shaken her head. It had never occurred to her that walking could be a mode of transport.

'You know,' Yumna said now, interrupting Mr Turner's reply, 'I'm becoming quite the walker myself!'

'Oh, is that right?'

She nodded. 'Yup! Norton is teaching me all kinds of walking tricks.' She pointed in the direction of Whitby Street. 'We went exploring after choir, and he was teaching me all these signs to watch out for, and all these sayings with wisdom . . .' Yumna cleared her throat and stood up tall, like she was presenting at assembly. She recited from memory:

'Beware of an oak, it draws the stroke,

Avoid an ash, it courts the flash,

Creep under hawthorn . . .' She paused, taking a breath.

'*It will save you from harm*,' Mr Turner said, completing the proverb.

Yumna smiled, although Mr Turner did not look as

pleased as she did. 'So you know it too!'

He nodded.

'It will save me if I'm ever caught in a lightning storm,' she said. 'Although, I first have to learn the difference between an oak, ash and hawthorn.'

Mr Turner smiled, although the expression did not reach his eyes. 'Don't worry about it too much,' he said. 'Just, avoid the tall trees and find somewhere protected – away from any water or metal – and you should be fine. Now, listen –' he cleared his throat, sounding awkward – 'What else did you do with this fella, Norton, was it?'

Yumna shrugged. 'Not much. Just walked around, learnt about the names of different birds, you know, nature-y things. He's like you.' She smiled. 'He said it's very important to *observe.* He knows that I want to be a detective!'

At this, Mr Turner looked quite nonplussed. Yumna misread his concern.

'Don't worry, I'm safe because it turns out *he* was the Moonlight Monster. There's no scary creature out there! It was just him, in a boiler suit . . .' She trailed off, realising she had veered close to revealing the secret again. 'Anyway, turns out he's a hept— a hetomo—'

She couldn't remember the word.

'A haematologist? Doctor of bloods?' Mr Turner ventured.

Yumna shook her head.

'Heptomologist?' Mr Turner tilted his head to the side, questioning his own suggestion. 'No, that one's made up. Hepatologist, perhaps?'

'No, no, no, none of those.' Who knew there were so many -ologists in the world? 'He is an expert in reptiles and amphibians.'

'Ah. Herpetologist,' Mr Turner hummed. 'Why is a herpetologist in Silverbrook?'

Yumna leaned in, unable to keep the secret.

'Well, he said that I couldn't tell anyone, but he's here because of the Maidstones.' She watched Mr Turner's expression change, pleased that for once, *she* had the gossip.

'Are you sure you can trust him?'

'Yeah, why not?' Yumna frowned, annoyed that Mr Turner was questioning her, rather than congratulating her on her excellent detective skills. She had solved the mystery of the Moonlight Monster, after all.

'It's just . . .' Mr Turner scratched his jaw. 'Didn't your father say the Maidstones were trouble?'

'Yeah— Well!' Yumna hitched her rucksack up her back and stepped back from Mr Turner's fence. She didn't want to have this conversation any more. Mr Turner was being like everyone else right now. Mean!

'The Maidstones are the only ones who have done anything nice for this village in ages. I know my dad doesn't like them, but –' she started to walk away – 'maybe I can think for myself!'

Yumna sulked off. She could hear Mr Turner calling after her.

'Yumna!'

He did sound apologetic.

'I didn't mean anything by that, sorry, Yumna, come back—'

But she'd had enough. If her friends were too busy with their magical whatevers and didn't want to talk to her, and if Mr Turner was jealous of her new – *what would be the best word to describe Norton* – mentor? Well, it was their loss. She was going to be a detective. She was going to email that address from the advert, tell them all about solving the mystery of the Moonlight Monster, and that would be that. A wonderful, exciting future awaited. *Inshallah.*

Yumna pushed open her front door, thinking about dinner and praying (in that order), then stopped dead in her tracks.

'Huh?'

Given her status as a social pariah, she had expected the kitchen to be empty. Her dad had said he would be working late, as it was Friday and he took time off for the midday prayer. But sitting at the counter was everyone in the group chat she had been unceremoniously ejected from. Sadeeqa, Nafisa and Sami.

Yumna couldn't believe it.

She had never expected to see them all here. In fact, this might be the first time she'd ever had this many friends visit her, all together, in her own home. Was this the moment they were going to bring her into the fold? Was there some sort of initiation process that she had to go through before she could get her own magic powers?

'What are you guys doing here?' She couldn't hide the hopeful note in her voice. They were here! They were going to apologise, to say they knew they were wrong for kicking her out of the group, for keeping secrets from her this whole time. They were going to tell her how important she was, how they were sorry they made fun of her.

In the face of their contrition, she would be magnanimous. She would be the bigger person. She would say, *'Sure! I forgive you! I forgive you all!'*

Nafisa stood up and approached Yumna with deep worry in her eyes.

'Cousin. We need your help.'

CHAPTER FIFTEEN

Yumna looked back at her cousin, then turned to Sadeeqa and Sami. Nobody wanted to meet her eyes. She looked back at Nafisa.

Oh.

This was about Kareem, and playing with fire, and all the things she hadn't been told.

Hope curdled in Yumna's stomach like days-old milk. They weren't going to apologise because they weren't sorry for how they treated her, they just needed her help. She crossed her arms.

'No, I'm not going to help,' Yumna said.

Nafisa couldn't hide her shock. 'What do you mean?'

Sami stood up from his perch, shuffling past Yumna to the door.

'I told you this wouldn't work,' he whispered to

Nafisa under his breath.

'Sami, wait!' Nafisa pleaded. But he was gone, lumbering away from the awkwardness without a backward glance. The door slammed shut behind him.

Yumna cleared her throat before she spoke again. 'I mean, you don't need my help,' she said. She hadn't meant to sound so dramatic, but some part of her did enjoy the power she felt, seeing panic rise in the older girl's eyes. 'You made that pretty clear when you kicked me out of the group chat.'

That's the ego you need to watch out for. She heard the voice in her head chiding her for lashing out, for matching meanness with bitterness.

Yumna saw Nafisa bite her tongue. 'C'mon cuz, don't be like that.' A pause. 'Please, you're the detective, right? You know how to find things, and people.'

Yumna weighed up her options. She was still hurt about being frozen out for the last few days, and getting kicked out of the group chat was pretty intense, end-of-friendship levels of intense. But then again, here they were, asking her back into the fold. Isn't that what she wanted?

'Kareem's still missing, right?' Yumna said, choosing peace for the moment. 'Like, properly missing? I think you need to tell the parents.'

'We don't need the adults,' Nafisa said. 'They'll ask too many questions.'

'Well, what about your magical powers? You can talk to birds and play with fire. Why don't you ask the sparrows if they've seen anything?'

'The birds?' Nafisa sighed. 'They talk such nonsense, man. They keep going on about not having enough worms . . .'

Are they getting up early enough though? Yumna amused herself with the thought as she opened the fridge. She was famished, after all that time walking through the field. Nature exploring was such hungry work.

She kissed her teeth. The fridge was empty.

'Pasta it is,' she said to herself, before turning back to Nafisa.

'Seriously though, what do you think I can do?'

Nafisa pulled a face. 'Aren't you the one who wants to be a detective? Can't you figure it out?'

'Figure what out?'

Yumna's father had walked through the front door without any of them noticing. Behind him, Sadeeqa and Kareem's father, alongside Nafisa's mother, filed in. The adults filled the small lounge area, crowding around the low coffee table. Mrs Nasir, Nafisa's mum, sank into the armchair, sniffling.

This was very odd. Yumna had never seen any of the adults cry, and Nafisa's mum was all about keeping up appearances.

Mrs Nasir was a nice lady, but she hardly ever showed actual emotion.

'Mr Sulaiman tells me Kareem hasn't been home for days. He missed Friday prayer, and he didn't show up to Taekwondo training either.' Her father's voice was stern, as he looked at each of the teenagers in turn, waiting for someone to provide an explanation.

Yumna could feel the tension in the room, thick and heavy. She tried to make eye contact with Sadeeqa, but her friend's head was down, her hands covering her ears. Despite everything, Yumna felt sorry for her. She did not look like she was having a good time.

Her father fixed his steely gaze on Nafisa's mother.

'This must have something to do with the Maidstones.'

Nafisa's mother shook her head, fear gleaming in her eyes.

'It can't be, it can't.' Mr Sulaiman whispered prayers under his breath. He looked frightened.

Abdullah turned to Nafisa. 'I saw you talking with Hector. What did you say to him?' He was speaking quietly, but there was a coiled fury in his voice, the quiet tone of years of unexpressed pain and hurt. Yumna had never heard her dad speak in this way. Her father addressed his next words to his sister-in-law. 'Did you not tell her to *stay away from the Maidstones*?'

Nafisa shook her head. 'I didn't say anything, Uncle, I swear, Mr Maidstone's got nothing to do with this.'

'He's got EVERYTHING to do with this!' her father exploded. Nafisa stepped backwards, flinching, and the room cowered in response. His voice was filling the air with emotion, his rage almost a physical presence in the room. 'You children know NOTHING about what they've done!'

This was too much.

'Baba, what's wrong?' Yumna ran to her father and grabbed his hands, trying to look him in the eye and calm him down. He was trembling, she realised. Her father was trembling, and it wasn't just with anger, it was with fear. *Why were all the adults afraid of the Maidstones?*

'Baba.' Yumna stepped back, releasing him from her grip. 'Why are you so upset? What did the Maidstones do?'

Abdullah shut his eyes and took in a long, deep breath. He took another, then another, filling his belly before opening his eyes. He moved to a space on the couch and sat down like a man much older than his forty or so years. Worrying about the Maidstones had aged him.

He tapped the space next to him on the sofa.

'Come, sit down,' he said to Yumna. 'Nafisa, Sadeeqa, you too. Come, join us.'

As the trio settled in, he looked at the other adults.

'It's time,' he said. 'The children need to know.'

Nafisa's mum let out a whimper of dissent. 'This is not what we agreed,' Mrs Nasir said.

'The situation has changed,' he replied. 'Given Kareem's disappearance, so soon after their arrival . . .' He looked up at the flaky ceiling, searching for the right words. 'It is connected. It is all connected.'

'Sadeeqa, has anything been happening to you?'

Mr Sulaiman was looking at his daughter, his expression unreadable.

Sadeeqa looked up, sunglasses still covering her face.

'Has what been happening to me, Abo?' Her voice was flat, emotionless. Yumna couldn't tell what her friend was feeling, but she could see Sadeeqa's dad struggle with the words.

The sound of Sadeeqa's breath filled the quiet room, shallow and fast, as they all waited for her father to speak. The quiet stretched and Mr Sulaiman shook his head, unable to answer. He regarded his daughter with despair in his eyes.

'I'm so sorry, Sadeeqa,' is all he could say, his voice low, defeated. It was painful, Yumna realised, listening to an adult speak in this way. It felt wrong, somehow. They were meant to know the answers, to help, to fix things. They weren't meant to screw up and then be sorry.

'Do you know what has been happening to me, Abo?' Sadeeqa's voice was angrier now, the hurt replaced by hostility. 'Have you known this whole time why my mind is full of voices and my eyes are like this?'

Sadeeqa ripped her sunglasses off. Her all-white eyes stared out at everyone, demanding their gaze, their attention. Mrs Nasir gasped, hiccupping through her tears. Mr Sulaiman averted his gaze, and Sadeeqa stood up, furious at her father's reaction.

'Look at me, Abo! Do you know why this is happening?!' Yumna became aware of a loud buzzing from outside the house. It was like the sound of a large wasp. She looked around the room, searching for the source of the noise.

Sadeeqa was raising her voice now. 'Do you know why Kareem has disappeared? Is it your fault?!'

It wasn't a single wasp, Yumna realised with horror, as she looked outside the window. It was *hundreds of them.*

'Sadeeqa!' Yumna yelped. 'Stop, look at what you're doing!'

Sadeeqa turned to stare at Yumna. Her friend looked powerful, and terrifying. She stood tall and lithe in her black abaya and hijab, all-white eyes glowing magically against her dark skin. The edge of her mouth was crooked up in a small, sly smile, one Yumna had never seen before. It looked like . . . Yumna didn't want to finish the thought.

'Sadeeqa,' Mr Sulaiman begged.

'Did you call them?' Nafisa asked. She appeared struck,

not by Sadeeqa's control of the wasps, but the scale of it. '*All* of them?'

'Sis . . .' Yumna quivered, wondering if Sadeeqa would remember her terrible fear of wasps. 'Please . . .'

Sadeeqa shut her eyes.

In an instant, the room was filled with the overwhelming buzz of thousands of wasps. The angry droning consumed their senses. Mrs Nasir twitched and screamed, while someone – Yumna couldn't see who – fled the room. Yumna, her heart in her throat, beating fast like the wings of a hummingbird, shut her eyes and prayed.

They were inside.

CHAPTER SIXTEEN

'Sadeeqa!'

Yumna wasn't sure who yelled her friend's name out, but it made no difference. The buzzing grew louder in her ears. She could feel her chest constricting, like a band wrapped around her chest pulling tighter and tighter, crushing her ribs. Her lungs didn't have enough space to expand, she couldn't get the air down, she couldn't breathe . . .

Don't panic.

Easier said than done.

Focus.

With her eyes closed, Yumna raised her attention from the lack of air in her chest to what she could hear. *Pinpoint the closest sound you can hear*, Norton had said to her when they went exploring in the field. Buzzing, that was the closest sound to her ear. It was scary close, but she knew she couldn't afford to move or wave it away. That was a surefire way to a burning hot sting, then a trip to the hospital for them all. How on earth would they explain all five of them being covered in wasp stings?

Now, concentrate on the sound furthest away.

Yumna extended her awareness out. Past the whimpering of Mrs Nasir, past the *chk chk chk* of the wall clock. There was a hum, probably from the fridge. In the far, far distance, she could hear the bleat of a sheep, or was that her imagination?

The loudest sound though, the one her awareness snagged on and wasn't able to move past, was her father's voice. He was reciting Surah al-Nas from the Quran. It was a short surah, an easy one, one Yumna knew by heart, and often recited while she was praying, because she liked its rhythm.

Yumna began to whisper the surah under her own breath.

Qul a'uthu birab bilnas . . .

Abdullah repeated the surah, over and over, and soon enough, everyone in the room was repeating the words. Yumna knew the meaning of the verses. She thought about what the words meant as their repetition filled the room, seeming to quieten the buzzing, seeming to soothe the loud *zin* of the wasps.

I seek refuge with Allah, the Lord of humankind

The King of humankind

The God of humankind
From the evil of the lurking whisperer
Who whispers into the hearts of humankind
From among the djinn and humankind . . .

It felt like forever, but by the time the wasps had left and everyone had calmed down, only an hour had passed.

Nobody spoke, but they all watched the last wasp fly out of the window, the loud buzz still echoing in their ears. Sadeeqa had sunk to her knees, limp and tragic like a deflating balloon, and everyone else began to move, slowly easing motion into their joints, breathing. Mr Sulaiman cleared his throat as he approached his daughter, careful and cautious like he was approaching a predator. He spoke with a soft, soothing voice.

'Come, my darling. Please . . .'

Yumna placed a tray on the table and began to hand out cups of sweet red tea. Mr Sulaiman looked haunted, his shoulders drawn up to his ears and dark shadows smudged under his eyes. Mrs Nasir had regained her composure, Yumna noticed with relief, because she didn't know how much adult whimpering she could handle. A horde of wasps was one thing, but a crying auntie? That was an entirely different proposition.

Her father waited until everyone had a cup before beginning to speak.

'We owe you all an explanation,' he said. 'You, especially.' He met Yumna's gaze, sadness in his eyes. 'You need to know everything if we're going to find Kareem.'

'You have always asked me to tell you more about your mother, and I refused. I could not. We all thought,' he glanced at the other parents, 'that if we hid, if we never mentioned the past, or what happened, if we never told you the truth, we could protect you from the danger.' He sighed.

'But the danger found you anyway,' Mr Sulaiman sighed.

Her father remained silent. Yumna saw the muscle in his jaw twitch, his Adam's apple bob up and down, and then he spoke.

'A long, long time ago, in a village far away from here, two Muslims fell in love. They had both come from different corners of the world to start a new life, and when they met each other here, they knew their new lives had begun. They got married, and had children, and if this were a fairy tale, we would say, they lived happily ever after.'

He paused.

'The woman was human. But her husband? Well, he was a djinn.'

A cup hit the floor. The tea spilled out of Nafisa's dropped teacup, darkening the beige carpet, but nobody moved. There was stunned silence from the teenagers, until Yumna broke the spell, her confusion spilling over.

'What do you mean?' Yumna said. 'Is that even possible?'

'What is that, an interspecies relationship?' Nafisa looked half horrified, half intrigued. 'Is that . . . halal?'

Her father scratched his head, the discomfort showing across his face. He had never wanted to have this conversation, Yumna could see. Each sentence was painful. But why? It still didn't make sense. She pushed.

'What does this have to do with anything?'

'That couple . . . Well, Yumna, they were your great-grandparents.'

This time, it was Yumna who dropped her cup.

What did her father mean?

She was *part djinn*?!

CHAPTER SEVENTEEN

None of it made any sense. None of it could be real.

Yumna's father recounted the story in stops and starts, the teenagers listening with rapt attention. At some point in the night, Sami joined, called back in by Nafisa.

'We're finally getting answers,' she whispered when he arrived. As Yumna observed the closeness between them, she remembered the eyeshadow Nafisa was wearing at choir practice before the Maidstones had arrived. *Was there something more going on?* Yumna entertained the thought for a moment, before pushing it right out of her mind. She had other things to worry about!

Yumna stood up, trying to focus on what she was hearing. She looked around at everyone gathered in the room. The stoic Mr Sulaiman with his arm around his daughter Sadeeqa, who was still in the foetal position in the corner of the couch. Her own father perched on the edge of his armchair as he spoke. A fragile Mrs Nasir, flailing to keep her emotions in check. Nafisa and Sami, sitting on the kitchen stools, with cool, unreadable expressions.

'So, let me get this straight,' Yumna said, interrupting her father's narration. 'We're all the descendants of djinns?'

Her father nodded.

Sami spoke up, looking distressed. 'Uncle . . . I thought . . .' Yumna could tell the poor soul was not comfortable being listened to by so many strangers. 'Aren't djinns evil?' He looked around at everyone gathered. 'Are you saying we're evil?'

Yumna's father shook his head, standing up and pacing around the room. 'It's a common misconception, but no. Djinns are similar to us – some are bad, some are good, some are Muslim, some are not. Usually they stay invisible, so we can't see them. They have different powers to us humans and can take on different forms. Sometimes . . .' His voice hitched with suppressed emotion. 'Sometimes, they decide to appear in human form. Which means, sometimes, humans and djinns can fall in love.'

Yumna couldn't believe she didn't know what *species* she was any more. This was *weird*. Thank goodness she had never sent her DNA to an ancestry testing place, what would the report have said? 85% Nubian, the rest some sort of alien?

'OK. So, we are all related to this community of Muslim djinn-human families that once lived safely and happily in a village?' she clarified. 'A place where everyone could use their powers openly?'

'That's right,' Abdullah said, drawing his daughter's attention back to him. 'Some djinn powers are connected to the natural world. Flora, fauna, the elements. Some people could talk to animals, some could make plants grow in whatever way they wanted. Some could manipulate fire, wind, water, but also time, space . . .'

'It wasn't just some random faraway village, Yumna,' Mrs Nasir interrupted. Her father glared at his sister-in-law, but she pointedly ignored him, ploughing ahead. 'You've been there before.'

'I have?'

'You were born there.'

Yumna's eyes darted between her father and her aunt with confusion. He looked pained, Mrs Nasir unapologetic. She directed her next words to him. 'We said we would tell them everything, no?'

Yumna didn't understand. 'What is she talking about? I thought I was born in Hull!'

Her father took his daughter's hands into his own. Yumna noticed he wasn't able to meet her gaze.

'You were actually born in a village in Cornwall, habibti.

A village called Gadeem. You loved it there, ya Yumna,' he said, his tone wistful. 'We all loved it, your mother especially.'

Yumna's world was turning upside down in real time. She blinked rapidly, trying to process everything she was hearing. Her father continued to reveal secrets she didn't know were being kept from her: not only was she born in this magical village, but her mother's gift was one of the most powerful ever seen. She had been close to the djinns, had spoken to them and learnt from them, and was able to breathe life into being. 'She could create a sculpture of a bird, speak words to it, and watch it fly away,' he said, his voice shimmering with awe. Yumna felt like she was going to be sick. This was all too much.

'But when the Maidstones arrived . . .' he continued.

'You mean the same ones that have moved into our village now?' Nafisa interrupted. He shook his head.

'No. Hector and Sybil are related to them, but they're not the same people.' He cleared his throat, readying himself for the weight of what he was about to reveal.

'After Tobias Maidstone inherited the plot of land in our village, he made it his mission to restore the Maidstone name to its so-called "full glory". He was an ambitious man, Tobias. And . . . some believe, an evil one. Now, I don't think anyone is evil. What I do think is that he had something in his ear . . .' Her father made a *ws ws ws* sound.

'*Ws ws ws?*' Nafisa sounded confused.

'Think of Surat al-Nas,' Mr Sulaiman said. 'The Whisperer.' His voice was low, full of fearful memories. Yumna hated seeing the adults like this. It was not the way it was meant to be.

'Nobody ever confirmed it, or knew for certain,' he explained. 'But everyone in the village believed the Maidstones' power came from the Whisperer.'

The penny dropped for Yumna.

'The *was wasa*. The Whisperer. Isn't that . . . *shaytan*?'

His nod was small and slow, heavy with sadness.

'Yes, my dear. The whispers of the devil.'

Yumna heard Sami suck in his breath.

Tobias had made a deal with the devil. A deal that would bestow greatness and wealth in this world to the Maidstone name, but a deal that meant he – and all his family – would be forever bound to do the devil's work.

'The Maidstones were good at what they did, the shaytan made sure of it. They made money in every venture they ran, every business they built—'

'That's why they're building the supermarket!' Yumna burst out, before remembering that was top-secret news. Everyone looked at her, waiting for her to elaborate, but she shook her head. 'Sorry, it's nothing. Ignore me.'

Her father looked curious but dropped it. 'You are right to say they do have a large share in supermarkets, that is correct. But that's not where their main money comes from. Their main money comes from *land*. So, they did everything they could to acquire it.'

Mrs Nasir, her tears gone and her composure restored, joined Yumna on the couch and hugged her close. 'Your mother's family – my family – had been living there a long time,' she said. 'I had moved away well before this all happened, but of course I still talked to my sister, Amina. She told me about the Maidstones. They wanted to take our family land. But Amina didn't want to sell. It had been in *our* family for generations.'

'None of us wanted to leave,' her father continued. 'We loved living there; it was our home. We had taken care of the land, and the land had taken care of us. But the Maidstones, and the Whisperer, they wanted what was ours, and nothing would stop them.'

The next part of the story was so predictable, Yumna thought. As expected, the Maidstones started blaming the Muslims – human or djinn – for everyone's problems. A bad crop, it was their fault. Prices rocketing, somehow their doing. These Muslims were outsiders, the Maidstones said. They were taking what wasn't theirs. They didn't belong here. They were *different*, and different was bad.

'We thought we were safe,' her father admitted. 'Because it didn't work, at first. We had been there for so long, these were our neighbours, our friends, and we believed they wouldn't turn on us . . .'

Yumna felt a queasiness in her stomach. Why did she feel like she knew where this was going? Why did all these stories end the same way?

'Hatred is an easy seed to plant, Yumna.' This was from Mr Sulaiman. His voice was soft, gentle, wise. He was still beside Sadeeqa, who had unfurled from the foetal position, sitting quietly, taking it all in. Mr Sulaiman patted his daughter's knee as he spoke, a touching, caring gesture. 'It lies quiet, until the environment changes and the right fertiliser comes along.'

Yumna remembered something Norton had said, about a phenomenon called *seed dormancy*.

'A seed will just wait there, in the soil, until the right conditions for germination arise. It's a survival technique,' he had said.

Survival for whom?

'They poisoned the village against us.'

Yumna's jaw dropped. Not with surprise, but a sense of haunting recognition.

'By the time you were a toddler, we knew we had to

leave. Our home . . .' Baba's voice wavered. In that moment, Yumna hated the people who made her father feel scared. She *hated* them. 'It wasn't safe any more.'

'What about Mama? Why didn't she come with us?' Her voice was that of a scared, lost child. Yumna was angry, yes. But also confused and hurt. How had they been keeping this from her for her entire life? Why had nobody ever told her this before?

A single tear ran down her father's face. Yumna could barely hear his response.

'Amina, your mother . . . She bought us time.'

Yumna didn't understand.

'When they finally came for us,' Abdullah said.

'The Maidstones?'

'No, they would never get their own hands dirty.' A dark, knowing chuckle. 'In the end, it was the other villagers. They'd had enough poison dripped into their ears that they believed the lies the Maidstones had spun. They were good at telling stories, Yumna, so good . . . and eventually, the other villagers, they turned on us.' He rubbed his face, as if to wipe away the memory. 'It was the middle of the night, when they came . . .'

Yumna looked at her father, tears in her eyes.

'Amina wanted to stay. I tried to make her come with us, but she refused to leave.'

Yumna tried to imagine her mother, standing her ground against a mob. A street full of screaming people, armed with what – hammers and shovels and cricket bats? 'Normal' people, who wanted them gone, or worse. She tried to imagine facing the roar of hatred from those who you thought were your friends, and it made her sick.

'Your mother never blamed them, you know,' Nafisa's mum said. 'She knew it wasn't their fault, the other villagers. She knew the poison of the Maidstones was powerful, a toxin that only had one antidote.'

Her father shook his head. It was clear to Yumna that this had been something her parents disagreed on.

'Amina thought mercy was the only way. But I saw murder in their eyes.'

Finally, Yumna understood what their parents were trying to tell them.

'Are you saying the Maidstones are behind this? Behind Kareem's disappearance?'

Her father shrugged. 'I wouldn't be surprised.'

'There's no way,' Yumna countered. 'They've done nothing but be nice to us and everyone in the village since they arrived.'

'They do seem quite nice,' Sami concurred. 'He smiled at me . . .'

'Of course. That's how they get everyone onside,' her

father argued. 'Either way –' he turned, dismissing Sami and Yumna's observations – 'I've decided. We've got to make plans to leave.'

'We can't leave Kareem!' Sami protested.

'You cannot be so cruel,' said Mr Sulaiman. 'We cannot abandon my son.'

'You're joking me,' was Nafisa's response, bolstered by glowering silence from Sadeeqa.

'Baba!' Yumna thought her father was better than this. How could he possibly suggest they run away, leaving Kareem behind?

All their voices overlapped. Her father put his hand up for silence.

In the quiet, Nafisa spoke. 'If he's really been taken by the Maidstones, then he needs all the help we can give him—'

'If he's been taken by them, we have no chance.' Her father sighed.

Yumna was perturbed. This was not what she had expected. 'I thought the whole point of this story was to prepare us for what we were going to face. To give us all the information to be able to figure out where Kareem is.'

'The point was for you to understand what we're up against.' His tone was final.

'*We* are the ones with the power.' Sadeeqa's voice boomed

through the room, and everyone turned to face her. She rose from the couch like a python, slow and deliberate, hypnotic and lethal.

'How dare you ask us to run away.' Her eyes flashed. 'My brother is missing, you think he might be in the hands of the servant of the devil, and you want me to sit by, quietly, waiting for— Waiting for what?'

Yumna couldn't believe her friend was talking to her father, a man who was Sadeeqa's elder, like this. But Sadeeqa didn't seem like herself. It was like the act of using her power made her bigger, stronger, more confident.

Yumna and Nafisa exchanged glances. *Whoa,* Nafisa mouthed to Yumna.

I know, right? Yumna mouthed back.

Despite everything, Yumna was just glad that she was talking to her friends again.

'If you all want to pack your bags and disappear like frightened cowards, that's fine,' Sadeeqa hissed, her voice like a rattlesnake's warning. 'But me and my friends,' *the din from outside was growing again,* 'we're going to save my brother.'

With that, Sadeeqa walked out the door.

CHAPTER EIGHTEEN

The next morning was market day.

'There is no way I am letting my daughter perform,' Mrs Nasir said, as stalls were being erected around her. The green square in front of Shington Hall was a flurry of activity, and Mrs Hardy had been up since dawn, preparing for what she hoped was the first of many performances. Yumna noticed patches of sweat darkening the armpits of her copper silk dress.

She must be stressed.

'What do you mean?' Mrs Hardy replied, horror colouring her cheeks. 'You can't just pull her out now. Nafisa is the star of the show, there's no choir without her!'

Yumna, who was standing in the clump of families behind Mrs Nasir, noticed the other chorists bristle at the implied insult. They were all standing on the edge of the green, watching the drama unfold.

'A child is missing,' Mrs Nasir said, her voice heavy. 'And it feels like nobody in this village seems to care. How can Nafisa be singing when we should all be out searching for Kareem?'

Sybil interrupted, waving her hand dismissively. 'Kareem's not a child; he can look after himself.'

'He's only sixteen,' Mr Sulaiman said, pushing back. But to Yumna's disappointment, nobody was listening. They were paying attention to Sybil. Yumna wondered if this was the power of the devil at work. It usually took years before anyone paid attention to a new villager's opinion. But this newcomer seemed to hold sway over the crowd.

'If you're so worried, why haven't you reported it to the police?' Sybil responded. 'Unless you think it'd be a waste of police time . . .'

Yumna had thought the same thing last night, but deep down, she knew the answer to that. Their parents didn't trust the police, and nobody thought the local force would take Kareem's disappearance seriously. Also, how on earth were they meant to talk about his powers without being laughed out of the police station?

Even so, Yumna was finding it hard to believe that the Maidstones were *evil*, as her father had argued. Sure, they might be related to the evil family from Gadeem in Cornwall, but you couldn't lump everyone from the same family together, could you? Kareem and Sadeeqa were just one example – completely different people, who had very different plans and ambitions in life. Maybe not every Maidstone was as hellbent on power as Tobias.

All that said, Yumna couldn't help but pay close attention. Would they give something away? Would her detective senses pick up something everyone else had missed?

Mr Sulaiman continued to protest, asking people to help search for his son, but he was ignored. Nobody ever listened to Mr Sulaiman. Not in this village, anyway.

After Sadeeqa's abrupt exit last night, things had gotten awkward. Mr Sulaiman had run out after his daughter. Mrs Nasir left the house without uttering another word, dragging her daughter out in a vice grip, anger palpable. Mrs Nasir must have confiscated Nafisa's phone too, Yumna realised, because none of her messages had been delivered. Sami, who lived in the next village with his uncle, crashed on their couch, but he wasn't up for chatting despite Yumna's best efforts. She was so curious about his firepower, but the only sign of magic she noticed was that his farts smelt like burnt charcoal.

Yumna had hoped that the adults would know what to do, combining forces to find Kareem, but it looked like they could be as petty and scared as anyone else. She tried not to be too disappointed in her father, but she didn't know how to feel. All she knew was Kareem was missing, and if nobody else was going to try and find him, they needed to do something about it.

'Is there some trouble here?' Yumna heard Hector ask Mrs Hardy. He had come to see what the commotion was about. 'Are these people bothering you?'

There was murder in their eyes.

Was there murder in Hector's eyes? What exactly did that look like?

Mrs Hardy looked startled by the suggestion, but before she could respond, Hector spoke again.

'Don't you worry about a single thing, Mrs Hardy.' He brought his hand to his chest, like a benevolent ruler. 'We'll get rid of these rabble-rousers.'

Mrs Hardy looked baffled. 'No, no, it's not—'

Hector smiled, broad and kind. *The kindness of a wolf to the keeper of the henhouse.*

'Trust me.'

Hector called over a security guard, switching to a tone of authority.

'Escort these people off the premises, please.'

It all happened so quickly that none of them knew how to respond. Not Mrs Nasir, who was one of the most law-abiding, village-loving people in Silverbrook. Not

Yumna or Nafisa, who were following the conversation ping back and forth like a tennis match. Not Mr Sulaiman, or Abdullah. One minute, they were talking to Mrs Hardy about the choir, the next, they were being frogmarched off the green.

Yumna's mind raced. There had never been security at a market before. It was a local village market, why would they need security? But there were three men in yellow vests, just 'doing their job' and another man in a leather jacket who looked familiar . . .

'Norton!?' Yumna said, as the nerdy man she had gone nature exploring with pushed Abdullah's shoulder. 'What are you doing here?'

'Norton works for us,' Hector said in Yumna's direction. 'He's a loyal servant of the Maidstones, and has been with the family for many years.'

Yumna couldn't believe it. She shrugged away from the security guard that was trying to move her along. Getting in between Norton and her father, she looked up at the man who less than 24 hours ago, she would have considered a new friend.

'Norton, what are you doing here?'

Norton shrugged. 'My job, lassie.'

'I don't understand – you told me . . .' She searched for the words, then spotted Mr Turner in the market crowd.

He turned before she could register his expression, and this small movement snapped something in Yumna. Why was it that every single person she relied on had lied to her, shunned her, turned away from her?

'ARE YOU EVEN A HERPETOLOGIST?!'

The market fell quiet. All eyes turned to the scene: the three Muslim families, surrounded by security guards, being ushered off stage.

Then, in the distance, the sound of a thousand buzzing insects began to rise . . .

CHAPTER NINETEEN

'Why are we letting them push us away?' Sadeeqa hissed.

She had been out all night searching for her brother, to no avail. Yumna could see her friend was exhausted, but she knew Sadeeqa wasn't giving up. This was the Taekwondo champion in her – the person who wouldn't take no for an answer, her best friend who never backed down from a fight.

You don't know who you've upset, Yumna thought, feeling almost sorry for the Maidstones.

Sadeeqa was standing at the edge of the green, surrounded by onlookers. She ripped the sunglasses from her face, all-white eyes flashing. A quick Taekwondo move and she was free from the grip of the security guards. She strode towards Hector. Yumna tried to call out, but Nafisa's glare silenced her.

'Face me,' Sadeeqa demanded. Her voice was loud, echoey and strange, like she had the voice not of a single person but of hundreds, millions of creatures. The buzzing grew louder, roiling into a thunderous din. It came from beneath their feet, from the deep in the soil and filled every inch of the air.

Sadeeqa was calling an army.

Hector was walking away from Sadeeqa, guiding Mrs Hardy towards Shington Hall. The conductor glanced over her shoulder at Sadeeqa and visibly paled. She tapped Hector on the shoulder, but he ignored her, until—

'We shouldn't be running when *we* are the ones with the *power*!'

A sudden wind billowed Sadeeqa's abaya wide open, like a cape. She looked frightening and formidable, and Yumna didn't quite know how to react to this version of her friend. She looked at Nafisa again, but her cousin's attention was squarely on Sadeeqa. All the villagers and visitors who had been setting up the market had stopped working, looking up and muttering about what was happening. This wasn't just a couple of troublemakers being told to leave. There was something bigger brewing, something outside of their understanding.

Sami came up to stand beside Sadeeqa, lifting his hands up to chest height, as if in prayer, before a ball of flame burst into life between his palms. Nafisa also stepped forward to join Sadeeqa and Sami, but her mother grabbed her by the arm, pulling her back. Nafisa grimaced, but then Yumna noticed her cousin and her aunt exchange a long glance. They had a whole conversation without words, until Nafisa's face dropped and she relented.

Would she have been able to have those type of wordless conversations with her own mother, had it not been for the Maidstones? Yumna shook her head. No time for such thoughts now.

Hector and Mrs Hardy were facing them again. Mrs Hardy looked terrified, confused by the sight of the teenagers wielding power like she had never seen before. Hector's face was expressionless, unreadable.

The perfect upper-class Englishman.

Behind them, one of the choir members, the retired doctor, emerged through Shington Hall's front door.

'What is taking you all so long—' She stopped, speechless. Sadeeqa had surrounded the green square with a wall of angry, noisy insects, buzzing and snapping and circling them like prey. Beside her, Sami was flicking fireballs in the air, muscles bulging, his eyes glinting amber. Most of the people who were working the market stalls were quiet, standing so still it was as if time itself had been frozen. The scene was altogether eerie, surreal.

Sybil cleared her throat. Yumna wondered how this woman was going to explain what everyone was clearly seeing.

'It must be climate change,' she said, looking at her husband and shaking her head. 'I keep telling people, if we don't pay attention to our energy consumption, this,' she threw her hands up at the insects, 'this is what we will get!'

'And this one here.' She pointed at Sami. 'Looks like he's practising to join the circus.' She *tsk tsked*, eyeing the circling insects. 'It's downright biblical, don't you think?' She turned back to the hall. 'Once the weekend is over, I will be reporting this to the committee. This is the kind of thing we have to put up with in the countryside and they simply do not care—'

'Enough!' Sadeeqa thundered. Sybil stopped, turned back, and stared at the teenager in shock.

'Excuse me, are you talking to me?' When Sadeeqa didn't reply, Sybil scoffed in disbelief. 'Have you completely lost your senses? That is incredibly rude, and only hours before our performance together.' She raised her eyebrows, seemingly unperturbed by the all-white eyes and insects.

'*Where is my brother?*' The question reverberated, as if it had been asked into a canyon. The pitch of the insect din increased, Sadeeqa's anxiety reflected in the creatures she was controlling.

'No need to yell. Goodness!' Sybil replied. 'He's probably out somewhere drinking or vaping or whatever teenage boys do these days.'

'He's been gone for days,' Mrs Nasir said.

'Also,' the timing felt wrong but Yumna had to set the record straight, 'he doesn't drink. None of us do.'

Sybil scoffed. 'I know plenty of Muslims who break the rules and have a tipple every once in a while. You wouldn't be the first religious community to have a few wayward souls.' Sybil brushed an imaginary bit of lint off her shirt. 'I'm going back inside. Hopefully whatever this is,' she waved her hand again, 'sorts itself out soon.'

And with that, she was gone.

Taking advantage of Sadeeqa's momentary distraction, Yumna hurried to her friend's side, clasping her hand in her own.

'Please, Sadeeqa, please calm down,' she said. Hector and Mrs Hardy were in furious conversation, while their parents huddled behind them.

'No,' Sadeeqa hissed. 'My brother is missing, and *HE* –' she raised a finger and pointed at Hector – 'had something to do with it.'

Hector looked up from Mrs Hardy and frowned at the accusation. 'I've done a lot of things in my life, but I have nothing to do with your brother's disappearance. What would I want with him anyway?'

Yumna suddenly remembered something. It had been forced to the back of her mind with everything else going on, but now—

'Hey, Naf,' she said. 'Where's Norton?'

Nafisa shrugged, annoyed at the random interruption. 'How should I know? What does it matter, anyway?'

'Well, he was there the night Kareem disappeared, wasn't he?'

Nafisa shook her head.

'What are you talking about?' Sami asked, as the fire in his palms extinguished with a crack.

'I saw him join you guys that night,' Yumna said, her mind hurriedly trying to connect the dots. 'I thought you invited him, and I did think it was kind of weird you'd invite some old dude but . . . Anyway, I was upset because he got to go, and I didn't even get an invite . . .'

Nafisa rolled her eyes. 'I told you—'

'That's not the point of the story. Point is –' Yumna's detective brain was kicking into gear. She narrowed her eyes at Hector – 'You might not have anything to do with Kareem's disappearance, but Norton definitely did, didn't he? And he works for you?'

There was the tiniest hesitation before Hector spoke.

'I haven't the faintest clue as to what you're talking about.'

It was such a tiny moment, barely a hair's width of a pause, but Yumna heard it. She was on to something.

But before she could launch into a speech, demanding that he confess what he knew about Kareem's disappearance, Hector moved. He made his way into the centre of the green and climbed up on to a stack of wooden pallets, turning it into a pulpit. The insects were still buzzing, the air was still crackling with tension, but Hector's voice rose above it all, as if delivered to each person's individual ear.

The was wasa . . .

'Fellow villagers,' Hector said, his arms wide, suit crisp, demeanour charming. Yumna watched the people around the square relax, the tension in their shoulders and jaws ease, their attention caught and soothed by the delicate web of this man's power.

'I must thank you all for your kind welcome to the wonderful Silverbrook. It has been an honour, and a privilege, to come back to a place my family has long been connected to . . .'

That was a lie! But nobody seemed to care.

'. . . and you can rest assured that my wife, son and I will do everything in our power to bring safety and prosperity to this wonderful corner of England.'

A light applause pattered around the green. Then, like

a thundercloud passing across the sun, Hector's mood darkened.

'There are some, however, who are not invested in bringing safety and prosperity to our green and pleasant land. It is thanks to my enterprising right-hand man, Norton Times. Come here, Norton.' He waved the fake-herpetologist over. 'That I can tell you *for a fact* that *some* of the families gathered here today come with *nefarious* intentions.'

Norton avoided Yumna's eyes as she stared him down, still unable to believe that he had lied to her so blatantly. He said he had been looking for the newts! Now that she thought about it, did he say he wanted to save them, or kill them off so the development could go ahead? *Oh, Norton!*

'As many of you know, my family has inherited a significant package of land in this area, which does give us a say in those who might choose to live in the houses in this village.' A chill ran down Yumna's spine, and she heard her father muttering in Arabic under his breath. Was he praying, or cursing? She couldn't tell. But whatever Hector was going to say next, she was pretty sure it wasn't going to be good.

'So, in light of this, here is my proposal. This evening, after the conclusion of market operations, we will gather in Shington Hall for a vote.'

‘A vote on what?’ Yumna barely recognised her father’s voice, so thick with emotion.

‘A vote on whether or not your families should be allowed to stay in Silverbrook village,’ Hector said, his smile broad and menacing, like that of a wolf.

‘We’ll see you all tonight.’

CHAPTER TWENTY

Back at Yumna's house, the closest to the square, the adults were in complete panic mode.

'We've got to start packing,' her father said, running around and randomly putting things into a holdall. 'Has anyone seen the passports?'

'Baba.' Yumna tried to calm him down, but he wasn't listening.

'Cash, anyone have cash on them? I might need to go to the ATM . . .'

She hadn't seen him like this before. Or, maybe she had? Something in the stress of his voice reminded her of a much scarier time.

'Surely they won't come for us,' Mrs Nasir said, but Baba looked at her with a grave expression.

'That's what we thought last time.'

'Where is my son? Where is my son?' Mr Sulaiman was pacing in the kitchen. 'Yumna.' He looked up. 'What was it you were saying about Norton?'

'Oh.' She was glad of something to focus on, because the anxiety of the adults was starting to stress her out. And she couldn't stop thinking of Sadeeqa's question: why were *they* running, when they had powers?

Sadeeqa was laid out on the sofa, fast asleep. Turns out using magic is exhausting. Her friend needed to nap every time she used her powers.

'I saw him going into the woods, that night when Nafisa and Sami and Kareem were showing Sadeeqa how to use her powers.'

Mr Sulaiman hummed, thinking, then turned to Nafisa. 'Tell me again what you remember from that night.'

She shook her head. 'The weird thing is, Uncle, we don't remember much. One minute we were laughing, Sadeeqa being shown how to do an insect dance by this tiny spider, the next minute, I blacked out.'

Sami shook his head in agreement. 'It was weird. It was almost like someone cast a spell, one minute we were awake, watching Kareem majestically transform, the next . . .'

Mr Sulaiman shook his head. 'There are no spells in our power,' he said. 'That's a myth. Our powers are connected to the earth, the nature, our intention.'

'But they are working with the devil! What if shaytan taught them spells?'

Yumna sat next to Nafisa, who was flicking through an old, large book. It was the red leather-bound tome from the bookshop she had seen her cousin browse through a few days ago, although now that day seemed like ancient history.

'What are you looking for?' Yumna asked. The pages were filled with dense, cursive text and the occasional image of a creature, some familiar and some fantastical.

'Something that could help us find Kareem. This book has all sorts of information on the different types of power the djinns have, so I thought maybe it could tell us more on what Kareem's power could do . . .'

'He could turn into a horse, right?'

Mr Sulaiman, who was still in the kitchen, suddenly stopped pacing.

'What did you say?' He joined Nafisa and Yumna, kneeling down and placing his hand gently on Nafisa's shoulder. 'What did you say his power was?'

'Well, he could turn into a horse, like this beautiful golden thing, and he would disappear and come back in the blink of an eye, it was so . . .' She trailed off. 'He would talk about seeing all these different things, but he would never be gone for very long, so we thought he was making it all up.'

Mr Sulaiman's face brightened, and begging permission with his eyes, he took the book from Nafisa, flicking through it until he arrived at a double-page spread with a single word written in gold. '*BURAQ*'

'No . . .' Baba whispered. 'It's not possible.'

'But that's what the children are saying,' said Mrs Nasir.

'My son is the mystical horse?' Mr Sulaiman whispered. 'But, how? Is that even possible?'

'Perhaps he's not *the* horse, but a descendant of it. A creature that can change shape, and travel through both time, and dimension.'

Yumna watched the adults around her, as well as Sadeeqa, Sami and Nafisa, react in awe. They began to pore over the words in the book, wondering where Kareem might have actually gone, whether he had gone to a parallel world, or simply to another place in the same time.

She had a sudden urge to cry.

This was so unfair!

How come everyone else got powers and she didn't? Didn't she deserve to be special like everyone else?

She couldn't talk to any animals, her friends weren't really her friends, and she didn't even have a mother. Yumna wondered if *she* went missing, whether anyone would actually care. Would all these people gather around and fight for her, like she was fighting for Kareem?

Yumna muttered under her breath, rising from her feet. She was going to leave all this, sulk in her room.

Then, Sadeeqa's eyes flashed open. She made eye contact with Yumna, beckoning her over with a tilt of her head.

Yumna reluctantly shuffled over and leaned down to hear Sadeeqa's voice. Her friend was still exhausted but managed a few words.

'*Don't listen to the was wasa . . .*'

Yumna pouted. She hated it when her friends were right.

Back in her room and perched on the edge of her bed, Yumna swung her legs, thinking.

What could she do?

The parents were panicking, and they clearly weren't going to listen to reason.

Sadeeqa was knocked out, and Nafisa was in a world of her own right now. Sami – he wasn't even worth bothering with. He was good with fire but had the attention span of a flea.

She didn't have any powers. But she did have information . . . and she did have Allah.

Yumna scrambled to her feet and laid out her prayer mat. It wasn't the time for any of the prescribed prayers yet, Mr Sulaiman had already made them do Dhuhr and

Asr together. But she could just ask for help. For guidance. For something.

So, Yumna prayed. She said two rakaat, and during the final *sajda*, her legs tucked and body folded over, her forehead and nose touching the smooth material of the mat, she prayed. She spoke to her God like a friend, explaining the dilemma (though Allah already knew) and how she felt about it and how much it sucked that she didn't have powers (she understood that Allah knows best, but could Allah let her in on the plan at all?). She asked Allah to send Kareem back from wherever he got himself stuck and she asked for their safety, because she liked Silverbrook, and she didn't want to move, and Mr Turner was an excellent neighbour and she wanted this summer to be a success, so please, please, please, would Allah help a sister out?

By the time Yumna finished praying, she had a plan.

'Nafisa!' Yumna hissed, from the door of her room. She wanted to do this without the interference of the adults, but she couldn't do it completely alone. She needed information, information she didn't have enough time to collect herself.

Yumna pulled Nafisa into her bedroom and closed the door behind her. Then, she unlatched the window, opening it wide. They could hear the chatter of birdsong, the natural buzz of insects, the distant groans of livestock. This was country living, this was their home – and today, their home would help them find their missing friend.

'Can you call some of your bird friends?'

'Huh?' Nafisa screwed her face up. 'What for?'

'You know you can talk to birds, right? Flying creatures with excellent eyesight that can see literally everything happening on the ground . . . if Kareem's out there, surely they will have seen something?'

Nafisa rolled her eyes. 'Honestly, these birds are not worth speaking to. They've got nothing useful to say. They don't know anyone's names, they don't understand human behaviour. You should hear what they say about us!'

Yumna groaned. Although she was intrigued by the way birds saw things, this was not the time for it. 'C'mon, Nafisa, think! What's the smartest bird you know? Call them and we can ask them some questions.'

Nafisa grumbled, but she did as she was told. Yumna knew she would, her cousin was annoying, but not a fool. Nafisa perched on the windowsill, opened her mouth and began to trill.

Yumna gasped. Her cousin sounded *amazing*. The way she sang, it wasn't English words, or birdsong exactly. It was something in the middle, something that moved and warbled in the air, a sound unlike anything Yumna had heard before. But even though it was so unfamiliar, it felt . . . magical. It felt true. It felt *just right.*

Nafisa turned to face her cousin, her face a mask of boredom.

'Fine, yeh, whatever. I called Tayeb, he'll be here soon.'

'Tayeb? You already gave him a name?'

Nafisa sighed. 'Yes, he told me his name was Tayeb, which technically means "good, right" or "sweet" in Arabic, as you know. But I think he got called Tayeb because he talks too much, and people are like "OK, *good, right*, stop!"' She pursed her lips. 'He is annoying, but he knows what's going on in every corner of this village.'

The bird that sailed in had a wingspan so large it almost didn't fit through the window. It was mostly blueish grey with striking black wingtips and a sharp, curved beak. It moved with a regal, predatory grace. Yumna had never seen anything like it before.

'He's a hen harrier,' Nafisa commented, as Tayeb climbed into the room, settling his wings. 'No, you can't bring your girlfriend here,' Nafisa warned, watching as he eyed Yumna's bookshelves.

'They're very rare,' Nafisa explained. 'Almost extinct. So Tayeb here is obsessed with finding a mate so he can have kids and they can keep the hen harrier species going.'

'Oh my gosh,' Yumna said. 'That's so sad.'

Nafisa huffed, like she knew she was meant to be sad but had heard the story a hundred times before. 'I know, and I thought so too when he first told me. But the bird won't shut up about it, and I can't help him find a mate, can I? I don't know any good female hen harriers to set him up with. Anyway, what do you want to know?'

Yumna's instincts were right. Tayeb knew exactly what she was asking and pointed them in the right direction. Yumna appreciated his precise instruction, until she realised all the distances he was describing were 'as the crow flies' – or as the hen harrier glides he corrected. It would be much more difficult for humans to make the journey, but they would have to try.

'OK, let's go!' Yumna said, after she'd thanked Tayeb for his service and he'd hobbled back to the windowsill and flown off. Nafisa looked at her quizzically.

'Where?'

'Where Kareem is. Where we should have looked from the beginning. The Maidstones.'

Nafisa looked nervous at the suggestion. 'Breaking and entering? Shouldn't we just tell Mr Sulaiman and let him deal with it?'

Yumna stared at her cousin. 'You seriously want to let the uncles handle this?'

Nafisa's shoulders dropped. They loved their parents but, somehow, they both knew their elders would utterly bungle the situation if left to their own devices. The uncles would spend too much time arguing over every detail, they'd never actually get going. Mrs Nasir would be too emotional to help, and she was not the type to get her hands dirty, anyway. The only other option was Mrs Sulaiman, but she was too busy with the new baby to be an option. They had no choice but to handle it themselves.

Tayeb had told her – through Nafisa – how Glebe Manor had been changing since the arrival of the new two-legged-pale-walkers (the Maidstones). A lot of the creatures had begun to die, Tayeb complained, which he was annoyed about because Glebe Manor used to be home to the tastiest voles. But the trees and plants had begun to change in strange ways. They were acting like it was winter when it was still summer, losing their leaves and shrinking in size. That wasn't the only oddity either. There was a new addition to the farm: a big, yellow, four-legged beast that glowed in the dark and never seemed to eat. It had arrived a few days ago, Tayeb said, but he didn't have too much more information on it. Looking at the beast hurt his eyes, because it was like it was there, but it wasn't. What he *had* seen was the metal bracelet, wrapped around its legs. Tayeb hated metal bracelets. He'd seen them before, and they stopped birds from flying. If he could help the beast get out of the metal bracelet, he would.

Glebe Manor had indeed changed since the Maidstones arrived. Gone was the feeling of light and sunshine that Yumna so loved about this place, replaced with a sense of foreboding, of secrecy, of darkness. Somehow, they had already erected an enormous iron gate and were building a sky-high brick wall all around the premises, blocking the Manor from view. As they approached the house, Yumna saw what Tayeb had described, trees losing their leaves well before their time, trunks blackening with some sort of illness, or simply dying in shame. *Is this the price of dealing with the devil?* Yumna had no time to wonder.

Tayeb said the glowing creature was in the stables, which were all the way around the back of the building. They had to sneak in, find and release Kareem, and sneak out – all without being seen and without getting caught.

The three friends stood in front of the gleaming gate, thick and imposing, squeaking threateningly in the light wind. Sadeeqa had spotted them sneaking out of the house and insisted she join. They had left Sami with the adults, a decoy to keep the elders distracted while they carried out their operation.

The trio joined hands and prayed a small prayer. *Ya Allah, protect us.* Tayeb circled high above them, acting as lookout.

'We ready?' Yumna asked, looking at her friends in turn. They both nodded. 'Let's save Kareem!'

Sadeeqa and Nafisa switched into gear. At Yumna's request, multiple pigeons pooed all over every single camera on the Maidstone property, completely covering up the lenses and blocking their vision. Sadeeqa asked a few mildly poisonous spiders to tranquillise the guard dogs surrounding the house, 'only sending them to sleep for a few hours, not killing them!' When all fifteen hounds collapsed on the ground at the same time, Yumna shook her head in awe. These powers were wild!

But she had powers too. She knew how to pick a lock! But of course, the Maidstone front gate wasn't an old-school mechanical lock, it was a highly expensive digital alarm system.

'Guess we can just . . . climb over?'

Nafisa shook her head. 'Nah, no way. One of us will definitely fall, and break something,' she said, eyeing Yumna with what she thought was a rather unfair assessment of her climbing skills.

'Gimme a sec.' Nafisa let out a few trills, then began to

jog around the perimeter. 'Tayeb says there's a gap in the wall somewhere back here . . .'

By the time they reached the stables, both Sadeeqa and Nafisa were wiped out.

'You've run out of juice so quickly?' Yumna asked.

'Why don't you spend the morning giving instructions to animals, huh?' Nafisa said. 'Let's see how far you get.'

'Naf. That's a bit harsh,' Sadeeqa said, seeing Yumna's expression drop. 'You know she wishes she could.'

Nafisa sighed, putting her arm up on to the side of the stables. 'I know, I know. I'm just exhausted. Sorry, sorry.' She sank to the ground, and Sadeeqa joined her, leaning against the wooden beam of the building's structure.

Yumna waved her hand. 'It's fine. Let's just . . . find Kareem.'

It wasn't fine, of course. It hurt like hell. But what was she supposed to do? This entire operation depended on their powers. Without them, without their gifts, she was nothing.

Tayeb sailed down and landed on the ground beside them, hopping excitedly. Tayeb bobbed his head at Nafisa, who rolled her eyes.

'Yeh, I don't care if you set up a nest here,' Nafisa said in English, before beginning to trill. Sadeeqa and Yumna exchanged glances as the pair exchanged chirps back and forth, the pitch of the conversation rising rapidly.

'Um . . . sorry to break up the party,' Yumna said, interrupting the tweet-off. 'But we don't have much time? We still need to find Kareem, don't we?'

Tayeb tilted his head, eyeing Yumna with what she suspected was hostility.

'Tayeb's just annoyed because he wants to scope the stables out for his nest, but I told him our priority is finding our friend. He doesn't quite understand the concept of *friendship* though, because he's a *bird*—'

Then: a noise that sounded like a horse, but also sounded like a teenage boy sighing.

'Kareem? Is that you?' Yumna called out. She looked at her friends. 'Can you hear that?' Yumna asked, but Sadeeqa shook her head. 'I can't hear much after I use my powers,' Sadeeqa explained. Nafisa sighed. 'Tayeb can go with you, I'm wrecked.'

'Go on, you got this.' Sadeeqa smiled at Yumna, the first proper smile they had shared in days. 'Find my brother.'

Yumna followed the sound of the neighing. The stables were separate to the main rectory, set all the way back from the building at the edge of the property and surrounded by grasping foliage. The two large sheds were both worse for wear and appeared largely unused. Yumna left Sadeeqa and Nafisa at the first of the buildings, larger and more modern but entirely empty, the stall doors swinging in the light breeze. She tiptoed towards the sound that was coming from the second shed, a smaller building with a collapsed roof. As Yumna pushed in the front door, she breathed in the thick smell of damp hay and poop. Tayeb, shuffling in behind her, let out an arch-sounding squawk. With an abrupt flap of his wings, he sailed out of the shed and perched on the roof edge. He would be the lookout.

The groans of heavy breathing were coming from deep within the stables. Although this shed looked like it hadn't seen a broom or light since the turn of the century, the hay smelt fresh. Yumna crept in, startled at every second step by shadows and creaks. The smell was stronger here, almost making her gag. *Oh gosh, Kareem. Is this where they've been keeping you?*

She walked to the last stall. As her eyes adjusted to the gloom, she could see a familiar shape lying on its side on the floor, grunting wearily. Its back two legs were shackled with thick, golden bracelets. As she approached, the creature's eyes opened wide with fear, then blinked rapidly as it took her in. Yumna swore she could see a smile on the horse's mouth.

'Kareem! Kareem, is that you?'

The horse's coat was a dull, mud colour, but as Yumna bent down to brush its neck, bits of dirt came off under her fingers. 'They've covered you in soil?'

The horse snorted in response, and Yumna began to brush away the caked dirt. With a few swipes, the light of the golden coat below began to glow through.

'Oh, it's you, it's really you!' she exclaimed. 'Let me get you out of these shackles . . .'

Fortunately for Yumna, these were old-school, mechanical locks. She had been practising her lock-picking skills via online videos for years, for just this kind of moment. Pulling out the lockpick set from her pocket, Yumna focused all her attention on the task in front of her. *Focus*, she told herself, as she used the thin metal tool to gently move the internal mechanism. *Breathe*, she told herself, like the friendly thief online had told her to do. *Every lock has a key . . .*

As she felt the mechanism pop open in her hands and Kareem's horse leg kicking free, satisfaction bloomed across her chest. Her face warmed with pride, and she let herself punch the air in celebration, before she began on the second shackle. *Betchya talking to a shrub doesn't feel this good.*

'Shh, shh, shh . . .' she muttered, as the glowing horse version of Kareem began to wicker and neigh as she worked. 'I've almost got it . . .' The lock popped open, faster this time. 'Look at that . . .' she said, unable to keep the self-satisfaction out of her voice.

'Yes indeed,' a voice came from behind her. She froze, her heart stopping for a beat. 'Look at that . . .'

She turned around. It was a voice she knew well, one she had hoped she was wrong about.

'Norton?' How had he gotten in without her noticing? *What happened to Tayeb?*

The friendly man from the BnB towered over them, his genteel expression replaced with a frightening, threatening scowl. Yumna noticed he was wearing the Moonlight Monster gloves, but why?

'What are you doing here?' she asked, not wanting to believe her eyes. She had guessed he might have something to do with Kareem's disappearance when Hector had hesitated earlier, but she didn't want to believe it. She didn't want to accept her new friend turning out to be the Moonlight Monster she feared.

'I could ask you the same question,' Norton said, walking towards Yumna with deliberate menace. 'Now, it's not you we want, little girl, so run along now. It's his power that we're interested in.'

Norton reached towards the horse with his Monster gloves, then cried out in frustration. In an instant, the horse had disappeared, only to be replaced by a naked and very terrified-looking teenage boy. Kareem had transformed back into his human form – but judging by his reaction, his memories hadn't come with him.

'What is going on?' Kareem asked, panicked. 'Where am I?'

'You—' Norton glared at Yumna. 'You removed the golden shackles?!'

'There's no time,' Yumna said to Kareem, ignoring Norton's questions. She picked up a rag from the ground, throwing it in his direction for modesty.

'JUST RUN!'

It turned out that even though Tayeb had not been able to warn Yumna, he'd flown straight over to Nafisa and Sadeeqa and told them the Moonlight Monster from the woods was *here*!

'He's scary, run, run, run!' Tayeb trilled, and Nafisa dragged her friend up by the arm as Yumna and Kareem ran towards them.

'We've got to get out of here!' Yumna called, her short legs pumping as fast as they could (*wishing she had worked on her stamina in the past week, instead of staying in bed!*). Kareem, jogging beside her and doing his best to hold the rag around his waist, wore a look of utter confusion.

'Will someone tell me what the hell is going on?'

From behind them, Norton's roar. Tayeb had flown back to the stables and begun raking at the man's face with his sharp, predator's claws.

'Later, we'll tell you later. Let's just get home!'

Off to Yumna's they ran. A short, plush hijabi, a tall, exhausted athlete, long-haired beauty queen and a mostly naked teenage boy. They were trailed by a collection of sparrows, a few butterflies and a very rare hen harrier.

A motley crew indeed.

CHAPTER TWENTY-ONE

Shington Hall was full. The entire village had turned out for the vote. Nothing like this had happened in Silverbrook's history, and even though most people didn't have strong feelings about the vote itself, they were here for the drama. There was a clump of farmhands by the drinks table, staff from the BnB nibbling on the canapés (Mrs Hardy always had emergency canapés) and even some of the grand old families from Eastbourne Lane had come to watch the show.

The hall had been set up for an assembly, with rows and rows of seats for attendees and a long head table at the front. Hector sat at the centre of the table, with Sybil on his right. Yumna was in the back row, in between Mr Turner and her father. Kareem, Sadeeqa and Nafisa were all back at their houses, recuperating.

'Order!' Hector called. 'Order.'

The room quietened down, attention drawn tight like a guitar string. 'I hereby declare this meeting open!'

'Let the games begin,' Mr Turner whispered to Yumna.

Bismillah . . .

Yumna stood up from her seat.

'I would like to say a few words before the vote.'

While her voice was confident, her knees were shaking violently underneath her skirt. *Bismillah*, she thought. *Allah, I'm counting on you!*

Hector had just concluded his speech, telling a similar story to the one at the market. Yumna couldn't believe how easily the lies just slid into the ears of her fellow villagers, like slugs into their ear canals, infecting their bodies without notice. It was almost as if he had done this before, or it was a tried and tested strategy. Well, it wasn't tested against *her.*

Yumna walked to the front of the room, slow and deliberate so as not to give away how utterly nervous she was. With trembling fingers, Yumna pulled out a piece of folded paper from her pocket. It was a speech she'd written for the vote after they had gotten home from saving Kareem. She hadn't had much time, but it was the best she could do. Maybe public speaking could be her superpower?

Facing the room, she cleared her throat and began to speak.

'My name is Yumna Yousif.'

She could almost hear the room sigh with misery. God, what was she doing? She sounded like a schoolgirl giving a bad English presentation, not a powerful force against the evil of the *was wasa*! Her knees shook more, and the tremor in her hand was so violent that she let go of the piece of paper and, frozen, watched it waft down to the ground.

There was pin-drop silence in the room. Or, paper drop. Because the entire room heard the soft sound of a lined sheet hitting the linoleum floor.

Hector cleared his throat from behind her.

'Right, well, if that's all then,' he began, but his interruption shocked Yumna into speech. She was *not* going to let this man run her out of her own village.

Pulling an empty chair from the front row, Yumna climbed up on it and faced the room.

Much better. They can all see me now.

She turned and pointed at Hector.

'*This* man wants you to believe he cares about Silverbrook village. He wants you to believe that me and my dad, my cousins and my friends, we do not belong. Well, he could not be more wrong.'

She took a deep breath.

You got this.

Mr Turner's eyes met hers from the audience, proud and

firm. Her father's were glassy with fresh tears, and although Nafisa and Sadeeqa were back at home, she knew her friends had her back.

'Has this man told you his plans to cut down the woods to make way for a new development?' A murmur ran through the room. There was nothing villagers hated more than a developer. 'That's right. And he's gotten that man –' she pointed at the wounded Norton, who had taken a seat in the front row – 'to KILL great crested newts so that they can open a SUPERMARKET!'

At this, a woman standing at the back of the room fainted, dropping like a fly.

'He called us hooligans, when his own employee went around attacking my cousin and her friends, and Kareem, who you all know and love from the store.' Kareem would say it was because of his good looks and grocery-related banter but Yumna knew it was really his kindness that endeared him to the village. He would help the locals pack their groceries and then carry them out to their cars, making them laugh all along the way. 'As you all know, Kareem has been missing for days.'

At this point, Mrs Hardy stood up from the crowd. She was rather unhappy with how this meeting was going.

'Yumna, come on now. Mr and Mrs Maidstone have done nothing but be upstanding villagers from the moment they arrived, have they not? After all, they are the ones who organised the choral performance at the market.'

'But that went terribly because my friends weren't even allowed to be in it,' Sami called out from the audience. Yumna hadn't noticed him in the crowd, but she was glad she had one more ally on her side.

Slowly, he rose to his feet, his soft voice carrying across the room. 'People only like them because they've got money. But money isn't everything.'

'How dare you—'

'The young lad is on to something there,' Mr Turner echoed. A few heads turned, intrigued by Mr Turner's defence of the families. 'If you're in a glass house, I wouldn't be throwing stones . . .'

'Mrs Hardy knew about Norton killing the great crested newts, by the way!' Yumna said, her voice now powerful across the room. 'She knows everything that happens here, right?' Murmurs of agreement from the villagers, everyone knew of Hardy's nosiness. 'I'm sure Norton told her! She aided and abetted the murder of newts!'

A thud from the back of the room, this time the swooning of a well-known newt lover in the village, Henry.

'This is absolute slander!' Mrs Hardy cried, but Yumna watched Hector give her the slightest of nods, putting her in her place. She took her seat.

'They've done so much worse too,' Yumna said. 'Stuff you couldn't even imagine.' She wanted to call them all out, every single one of them, but when she told Mr Turner of her plan, he had pointed out people probably wouldn't believe her. It was too wild, the idea of Kareem being kidnapped and shackled to the floor in Glebe Manor. But, Mr Turner had suggested, maybe there is a way to let the Maidstones know what you know.

Before any more could be said, Shington Hall's front doors whooshed open. Kareem walked in, paler than usual but fully dressed (thank goodness), flanked by a proud-looking Sadeeqa and a defiant Nafisa, Tayeb perched on her shoulder.

There was some confused muttering from the crowd.

'Is that the missing child?'

'Is that a hen harrier?'

But Yumna could only focus on Hector and Sybil, whose expressions had changed, frozen into unreadable masks. *Were they afraid?* This was her way of letting them know.

Behind Kareem walked in Mr and Mrs Sulaiman, with the newborn baby wrapped to her chest. They both looked haggard, but relieved.

Kareem stood tall and proud, a young Somali-British lad in his prime, staring Hector Maidstone down.

The hall went silent.

A single hand went up.

'Excuse me,' asked a villager. 'I have a few questions about the hen harrier . . .'

It had been a historic evening. The vote was struck down – and by a majority of the village too. Not a super majority, Hector had commented, but he was just being a sourpuss. It would take a long time for the village to trust him again, after they had learnt about the plans for the Big Supermarket and all the further developments. The Maidstones had lost this battle. But, her father reminded her that night, they weren't going anywhere just yet.

'It was nice though, wasn't it?' Yumna asked, as her father tucked her in that evening, the first time they'd both been home for their bedtime routine all summer.

Abdullah nodded. None of the Muslim parents had expected that the villagers would defend them, especially as the Maidstones had already begun to drip poison into everyone's ears. Mrs Hardy was a classic example: she'd known Sadeeqa and Kareem their whole lives, but the moment someone offered to renovate the Hall and fund the county fair, she was sold! But then, the couple from Peacock Manor stood up, talking about how Mr Sulaiman was the best financial advisor they'd ever had, and even though they kept offering to pay him more, he wouldn't take it.

'The most honest person I've worked with in my life,'

the man said. 'For years, I wondered if he was fleecing us somehow, but no, he's just that rare breed of human who has integrity.'

There were murmurs of assent from the gathered villagers, and a few 'hear, hears'.

'Abdullah is the same.' Another villager stood up, Yumna recognising him as a farmer from the outskirts. 'He's sorted out farms across Lincolnshire with affordable equipment and reasonable loans . . . and when times are tight, he's always understanding. I wouldn't do business with anyone else.'

'They might not be from around here, but we like having them.' This was from Mr Gareth, Yumna's boss. 'My family has been here since the eleventh century, as you all know.' Everyone knew, as Mr Gareth brought it up at every town hall meeting. 'So I know a thing or two about who belongs here. And while Yumna might need to work a little on her own punctuality with the paper round . . .' This elicited a laugh from the crowd. 'You're all Silverbrookian, in my view.'

Applause. Applause. *They applauded us.*

'So, we're safe here?' Yumna asked her father, as they walked home after the meeting, the crescent moon smiling down on them.

'Inshallah, my daughter. Inshallah.'

But something in Baba's voice made her wonder if he believed himself.

CHAPTER TWENTY-TWO

It was morning. The village was still and quiet, save for the occasional bursts of chatter from birds waking up, and sporadic bleats from sheep. Mist covered the ground, but it had already begun to lift.

Yumna sat on her bicycle, her eyes closed, breathing in the country air with relish.

'Good morning, young lass! I see you're making the most of your summer break!'

She grinned at her neighbour, coming out of his front door.

'Oh, hello, Mr Turner.' She looked him up and down. He was wearing 'normal clothes', a pair of jeans and a shirt. He looked a lot younger than when he was in his penguin suit.

'You on holiday?'

'Something like that.'

He smiled and glanced up at the hill. 'Shall I walk you up?'

Yumna nodded.

'How are you feeling about it all?' Mr Turner asked, as they wandered up the incline. It was getting easier every time she did it, even though she was still out of breath.

'I don't know. Good, I think? We get to stay in Silverbrook. But I still have so many questions . . .'

And no matter how much she trusted Mr Turner – after all, he was right on the money about Norton – there was so much she couldn't tell him. If he knew that Sadeeqa was controlling the insects yesterday, rather than it being some freak climate change thing like everyone seemed to be believing, what would he do then? Would he still be on their side?

She was glad at least, that things were back to normal with her friends. After she arrived home, she'd unlocked her phone to find an invitation to a new group chat, titled 'Team Tayeb'. It was the magic circle, plus her.

'Sorry,' Sadeeqa had messaged. 'We were all a bit . . . you know. But we love you, always, OK?'

That was all Yumna needed, and she had fallen asleep with a smile on her face, and dreams of riding a golden horse through the heavens.

★

'I do have something for you, Yumna.'

Mr Turner pulled out an envelope from inside his coat, handing it to Yumna.

She turned it over in her hands. It was nice paper, thick and creamy, and the stamp was a fancy one – although it hadn't been posted. She looked up for permission.

'That's all right, you can open it.'

She pulled out a thick card with a few sentences in loopy, handwritten script. Reading the text, Yumna gasped.

Congratulations, Sleuth! You have been chosen as the successful applicant for the role of trainee-detective at the Turner Private Detective Agency. Are you ready to start investigating?

The pieces started to fall together. She looked up at Mr Turner.

'You're the one who put the advert in the paper?!'

Mr Turner chuckled, the laugh creases around his eyes deepening. 'Indeed, young lass. Now, I must confess, I don't practise as a detective any more, but I was impressed by the letter you sent in, describing how you tracked down and solved the mystery of the Moonlight Monster.'

Yumna beamed. When she'd sent the email through, she

thought it was probably a hoax. No one was ever going to pay attention to her skills. But here he was, Mr Turner. Paying attention all along.

'Now. What is the next mystery you want to solve?'

She had so many questions: would she ever get powers like her friends? What would the Maidstones do now that they had failed with their development plans? What had happened in Gadeem? Yumna looked up to the sky. It was pale and grey today. It was a blank slate.

'I want to find my mother.'

ACKNOWLEDGEMENTS

To be a writer is to walk a solitary path, but to publish a book is to become a team player. Thank you to my incredible team: agent Molly Ker Hawn, editor Nazima Abdillahi, illustrator Arianna Bellucci for the brilliant cover, and all those at Hachette who helped bring *Silverbrook* to life. Shout out to Carole and Andrew at Glebe House in Muston for the charming hospitality and stories of village life, and to the Isle of Harris for its wild landscape and inspiration.

Completing this book would also not have been possible without the SoA Authors' Foundation grant, and I encourage all authors to apply!

Here's also to the Imams, Uncles and Aunties of my childhood, the ones who taught us the Prophetic tales, who shared their love of the mythological and the unseen, who cultivated in us a sense of curiosity, an appreciation of the unknown. And to all of you along the way who have taught me not to be afraid. Who have pointed to the strength within. Who stand in your power, be it magical or human. May Allah fill all your efforts with baraka, inshallah. Wa ya khawaja, thank you for always believing in me. Alhamdulilah.

Author Photo © Rory Mulvey

YASSMIN ABDEL-MAGIED

has published five books, most recently *Stand Up and Speak Out Against Racism*, named a Best Book of 2023 by *School Library Journal* and longlisted for the 2025 UKLA Book Award and 2024 SLA Information Book Award. Her previous books include the essay collection *Talking About a Revolution* and two novels for younger readers, *You Must Be Layla* and *Listen, Layla*. *Listen, Layla* was longlisted for Book of the Year by the Children's Book Council of Australia, and named a 2022 Honor Book for Children's Africana Book of the Year by the Center for African Studies at Howard University in the US. Her TED Talk on bias has been viewed over 2.7M times. Sudanese by birth, raised in Australia, Yassmin now lives in London.